FIGHTING FOR FOREVER

Battle Born MC- Reno

Book Six

BY

Scarlett Black

Cover Art by Opium House Creatives

WARNING: This book contains sexual situations and VERY adult themes. Recommended for 18 and above.

BLURB

Tank is shattered.

He lost the woman he loves and faith in his own MC. Together, they schemed behind his back and hid the truth from him. Even when all Kat's secrets are revealed, he wrestles with forgiveness and wonders if he will ever be able to trust her again.

The Black Widow.

That's the title Kat earned as she killed to survive after fleeing Mexico. Be that as it may, if she wants the MC's help to bringing down the cartel her only choice is to overcome her distrust in men.

Can Kat learn to let go and trust her feelings for Tank? Or will the past she can't escape destroy her and the MC?

CHAPTER 1

Tank

My heart explodes, I can't breathe, and my knees give away when I see her lifeless body in Spider's arms. It's all so fucking wrong that the pain is crippling my breathing. Life and feeling have been sucked out of me. My need to touch her prevails over my physical weakness, and I go to Kat. My hand is shaking as I reach for her, brushing the hair out of her face. Gently, I place a kiss on her lips before Spider takes her away from me and inside the building.

I blink once, then twice, while my mind catches up with what is happening. Rage, like a bull, overtakes me, and Blade, with Axl's help, tries to drag me back as I charge forward for her.

It feels like nothing in this world could keep me away from Kat. But *they* can, and do, by wrestling me to the ground as I fight them off. Every kick and punch is futile against their hold. I can't get away from the choking grip around my throat from Blade's arm. His weight drops me first to my knees and then my whole body to the ground.

Her long black hair sways back and forth with every step Spider takes with Kat in his arms. Every single one shatters my world more and more. The road scrapes and cuts into my face, as I'm being pushed against the pavement with the force of Blade's elbow to the back of my head. A single tear escapes as my forever and any chance I had at love are being stolen from me.

Axl and Cowboy pile on top of me as well, pinning my body down and keeping me from running after her. It fucking hurts like a red hot poker to the heart.

"Tank, stay calm, brother," Blade, the Prez, orders.

"Get the fuck off me!" I roar. "He's fucking taking her."

The sirens sound off in the distance, a warning that the cops are on the way to arrest us all.

"Tank, we have to get lost, *now*." Blade jumps off me, Axl and Cowboy do the same. I jolt up to my feet, ready to run in the direction of where Spider went.

The Prez halts me, his voice steady and commanding, "She isn't in the building, Tank. Follow us to the clubhouse."

Indecision wraps its ugly claws around my mind like in a fog. I do the only thing that feels right and run to my bike, cranking it on. The three of us race down the freeway, fleeing the cops before they can spot us. The farther out we get and away from the scene, the angrier I grow. Hate for the world and everyone in it spreads like a plague from within.

Blade and the brothers turn off the freeway, taking the ramp toward the clubhouse. Not me. I accelerate and keep pushing on. The road calls to me like a demon as the wind and sun beat down against my skin. It barely helps to contain the rage that has taken me on its wicked journey, a road I have never traveled. Riding to the only place I know I won't be found. Mine and Kat's cabin in the woods.

The journey here is faster than usual with the speed I'm traveling through the city and up the mountain pass. As soon as my bike is parked, I get off and take in the silence that is at odds with my inner turmoil.

I look around at the forest, sun and brush, feeling completely alone. The wind picks up and wrestles the trees and leaves. The sounds suddenly come alive with a bird's squawk and chirp in the distance, waking me from my trance. I stand there, stunned beyond belief and comprehension of what I am feeling or dealing with. Emotions play with my head all at the same time. Pain lances my body from the betrayal and deceit from Kat. The anguish caused by her death, though, is the strongest of them all.

My boots shuffle forward toward the front door of the cabin and I find myself standing before the bed we left unmade from the last time we were up here. When I claimed her.

Goddamn it, she was *mine*.

I glance at our mess of crumpled sheets and dirty towels left on the bed. They call to me, to wrap them protectively around me. I fall into a broken heap in the middle of it all, staring straight up at the ceiling. A faint smell of her wafts into my nose and it burns like a fucking torch on its way into my lungs.

I clench my eyes shut while the memories of us here torment my soul. Her raspy words of pleasure and promises to be mine.

Lies.

My soul battles between the truth and deceit. They paralyze and keep me a prisoner, caught in her web. My body grows lax and sluggish.

I've been bitten by the Black Widow.

"Tank, look at me," Spider shouts from the passenger seat. *My vacant eyes look up at him.*

"She is going to be okay."

I sit and stare at him. What could he possibly mean? She is going to be okay?

He shakes his head at me. "Tank, SHE IS GOING TO BE OKAY." He says it again, sounding exasperated.

"What the hell does that mean, Spider? She is dead.*"*

"She's not dead, asshole. I made her look that way." The *fucker has enough nerve to snicker at me.*

Fuck! My eyes pop open from the nightmare, startling me awake. My heart is beating so hard in my chest, it feels like I'm having a heart attack.

Somehow, I fell asleep. I think my body gave up and gave in from the intense struggle of conflicting emotions that had overtaken me.

Right now, my heart is beating only because it has to, whether I want it to or not. My hands rub over my face back and forth and I struggle to breathe through the hollow ache in my chest. Labored breaths do escape and I beg the world, "Please. This can't be happening. I wasn't ready for this."

Anxiety crawls inside of me, pushing for me to move and do something. Get out of here where it's full of memories of us.

I roll out of bed, stand up, taking a pillow and the sheet with me. I drop them to the floor without care.

I decide to shower and snap out of it before I figure out what to do and where I am going. The hot water spraying my skin does nothing to warm the coldness inside. Blade is no doubt freaking the hell out and has Spider looking for me. I turned my phone off at a gas station before leaving Reno. I didn't want anyone to find me.

I turn the shower off, water rolling down my skin, and I wrap a towel around my waist. Loss wants to pull me under, and I rest my hands on the sink in front of me, bowing my head, not wanting to look in the mirror and see the emotions written across my face. Hollow. I don't know this man.

It was bad when my parents disowned me, and it stung when Ava left me for another man. But this is gut wrenching. Some part of me will never recover. A big piece of me feels warped with it all. I don't know who to trust and I feel as if my brothers betrayed me, too.

In one day, I lost all that I had accomplished in my entire adult life.

I won't lie down in defeat, though. I push myself off the sink to find my clothes and put them on. They are dirty and soiled, just like I feel inside. I can't stay here because, eventually, the Prez *will* find me, and I don't want them here. Even in her death, no one can touch her. This is all I have left. There is no way I can go to her funeral either.

The only thing that matters is revenge. Matias, her husband, will die for killing her.

And it dawns on me that she was taken and killed. Had she left with him of her own free will, she wouldn't have made a scene for Tami to see. Kat was too smart for that. She would have taken off into the shadows. She left me a clue, but I believed my own lies and doubts.

What is my dark angel up to today? Even in death, she belongs to me, and only me.

CHAPTER 2

Tank

My cut slides over my arms easily as I contemplate my first move. A beat so evil drums in my body. A thirst for revenge and blood flows like a crimson river from within.

Grabbing my bike keys off the counter, I slam the cabin door shut behind me on my way out. The bike eats up the road like a demon possessed, on a mission. Seek, kill and destroy.

Once I am inside mine and Kat's house, I start looking around for signs with a set of eyes I have never had before. Nothing in here matters except for clues.

I wonder if this was the world she had been subjected to her whole life. A new understanding hits me like a sledge hammer, of who she had really been. A queen in the Cartel playing chess with life and death.

Even though I am raging from within, my thoughts and actions remain calm. Absorbing the feeling of a possessed demon from her, I feel it entering my soul, finding its match within me. A focus so sharp and deadly overtakes my mind. I see *her* now, the pain that had driven her for so long. I loved Kat, but now I understand the Black Widow.

Red is coating the world.

Like in a trance, I walk into the bedroom we shared, and contemplate where she would have left me clues. Taking my time, I scan the room first and look at the stuff from a different angle. What things had mattered to her and what things hadn't. What had been moved and what hadn't.

I smirk when it hits me. She wouldn't have hidden something so important on herself. The Black Widow would have hidden it where I would never look. In my belongings.

Turning around, my eyes examine my stuff, trying to get a feel of where she could have placed any hints. What would I protect without a thought? My guns and knives. Reaching under the bed, I pull out the large metal case. The weight of it scrapes against the wooden floor. I analyze every corner and remember in my head how I left everything in place.

Two guns are out of order, and I pick both of them up. Under one of them rests a small thumb drive. I grip the device in my hand and pocket it, only to leave the house and ride over to Tami's. She and Solo are gone, either out to work or, I am sure, on lockdown until Matias is killed. I sneak around to the back of the house and unlock the door. When Kat and I got this house for Tami, we made an extra set of keys for us, in case we ever needed it.

Peeking around, I find Tami's laptop on a small table in her room and sit down with it. The device springs to life with a picture of Solo, Tammy and their baby, Cash, on the screen. I push the thumb drive in and open the one file on it, a video recording. Kat's face pops up and my eyes water as I choke on the emotion ripping through me.

"Hey, Tank. If you are watching this, then this only means that either I am dead, or that we started the second phase. I'm sorry, baby. I couldn't tell you everything. I hope that you find me alive at the end of this, and that you understand the reasons for me not telling you everything."

Her face looks down at the floor of a room I have never seen. She takes in a deep breath, steeling herself for whatever else she has to tell me. My finger pauses the video and I look behind her, at the surroundings she's in. It's all metal and, barely into the corner, I see a garage type door. Is she in a storage shed? I push play again, ready to finish watching the video.

"I know that you are onto why I am here, and it is not for me. I have left you clues, Tank, that only you can find. If you made it this far, then you *do* know me and have listened. My hopes are that you save what I failed to do. Keep going, baby, and destroy this drive, for your safety and everyone else's."

I torment myself with her voice and the pain in it as I watch the video several more times. Her words and face are everything, and I memorize it all, locking it away, even if I die.

Kat wrapped me up in her web and injected herself inside of me. She is my poison and obsession. I realize that she said she might still be alive. Was Kat anticipating her own death?

So many questions and few leads to follow. I sit in Tami's room, with her laptop on my legs, completely confused about what any of this could mean.

Holding my breath, I dare to hope that she *could* be alive. I set the laptop back to where it was and go with what I do know. She needs her biggest secret of all to stay protected.

I have a hard time of letting her go, but I manage to break the thumb drive and throw it away in the trash outside. My gut tells me that I need to investigate that family in California that I already found. Also, she shot that video in a small metal room. First, I look up all the storage facilities and narrow it down. I start at the closest one located near our house. The Road Dog will hunt down and find the truth.

I know that what comes next will be a battle to the death. Or to bring back the dead.

Hours pass and I'm about to give up for the day, but I push on and pick the lock of the storage shed. It wasn't easy, but I managed to obtain a list of customers. Only a few on that list were female only renters. Only one was under the name of Emily Scott.

The sound of metal screeches when I push the door up. Inside, I'm taken by surprise at the setup before me. Computer monitors sit above a small desk, a cot, food, and Kat's black Tesla. Nothing else, no papers or boxes. It's very clean and minimal.

I sit in the desk chair, turn the computer on and wait for it to boot up. Fuck, I have to enter a password. I try one and fail. Desperation starts to creep its ugly head in. My cheeks start to heat, and I attempt the second guess. Incorrect.

If I don't get this right, I will be locked out for good. The Black Widow will wipe the drive after three failed attempts, I know it. I bow my head in desperation and think. Kat said I was listening to her and I *knew* her. What would she use? It would be something *I* would use, not her.

It is always the easiest, most obvious pick. Relaxing my muscles and closing my eyes, I think of her and a word strikes me. I type in *K-Love*, and I have entry. A confirmation that she was mine. She brings me to my knees, because Kat was listening to me, too.

I browse through all her files and emails to clients, and I see for the first time who she had really been in the shadows. Ready to move and kill to fill the emptiness she lived with.

Every job she took was to protect women or children. She took out men who were influential in law enforcement or who took bribes.

I search for hours and find that all these people she killed either had worked for an associate of the Cartel or a Boss under them. One at a time, she was taking down a piece of the Cartel empire until she was ready to go after the big boss himself, Matias.

Pictures of missing kids and documents of their families kill me. Kids that where stolen and taken into the sex trade, only for the people who bought them to die months or years later. Did Kat kill all these people? Was she righting the wrongs of her family?

I find a file that's detailed with information on Kat's lookalike, Korina, her twin sister, without tattoos. I check the date of the file and see that it was just right before we left for Mexico to kill Angel, Matias' brother. Kat has several photos of her sister outside of schools, talking to children and bringing them to her house. Under the guise of helping them, she lured them there only to drug them, then hand them over to Matias' men. They were used and sold for profit, like animals. Makes perfect sense now why Korina had never been allowed to marry or have a family.

My hands shake and my vision blurs from the murderous craze that takes over my brain. Kat barely spoke about her sister, and now I know why she killed her. Korina had been a puppet of the Cartel. Working for them and prostituting children.

Pictures of the man she shot with Korina on that night, Estaban, the right-hand man of Matias, litter the file. She killed them both and the baby that Korina was carrying. Now I know, *fuck me.*

This was how Spider tracked her down. He knew that she was killing anyone that had to be an associate of the Cartel. The last one in California had been a big buyer. He had purchased, sold and used kids for his pleasure. Kat was contacted by the woman who couldn't get justice from the cops. She killed off one of Matias' biggest buyers, taking a small piece of him at a time, without him seeing it. Just like that motherfucker did to us.

For a moment, a wicked smile creeps over my face at that thought. Kat used Matias' own strategy against him, something he wouldn't have seen coming. Smart fucking bitch. He will pay for what he has done to her.

Kat didn't tell me anything, but now I know everything. He fucked up her heart and, no doubt, did some sick shit to her. Swallowing past the lump in my throat, I continue looking through her files and memorize what I can.

I click in her browser, and a string of webpages she visited come up. I go through each one, and my heart stops when a video feed comes up, with signal from multiple separate screens. The family in California that I found before pops up on the big monitor. They are sitting at the table, praying together before dinner. I click to enlarge that image and they fill the screen.

A little boy with darker skin and dark hair is praying with his head down. I watch in fascination as he's doing it. He pops his head up and big brown eyes hit me in the gut.

Kat. He looks just like her with those eyes.

The last pieces of the puzzle come together, and I see it all clearly. She left him with this couple to save him. Matias may be already aware that he has a son with Kat. I suspect he does know, and if he doesn't find him, he will kill us all to get to him.

I know that I will die for this boy, too, because Kat sacrificed her life for him and other kids just like him.

Matias won't be stopped until he's dead. None of us are safe until his body takes its last breath on this earth.

CHAPTER 3

Spider

With Kat in my arms, I haul her off to my truck by myself, where I have Solo waiting for us out of sight.

"Take my bike back to the clubhouse," I order him.

The whole time, I keep an eye on the streets, looking for the Cartel. After Kat and I are safely inside, I call the doctor and peel out of there. The police sirens are getting louder by the second and our time is running out. As soon as he answers, I update him on Kat's condition while I weave in and out of traffic.

Panic is setting in and I need her the hell awake. This is some freaky shit. I'm not even sure she's alive after the impact of the car crash and what Matias might have done to her. He could have choked her to death for all I know.

It takes me forty minutes to get to the abandoned mine. We all agreed before this started that she couldn't go to the hospital if anything happened. Matias would locate her easily there, and it would obviously be the first place to look.

Kat's head is bobbing side to side with every turn and bump on the old dirt road. As soon as I reach the mine, I slam my foot on the break, lurching the truck forward. It skids sideways and dust flies around us like a cloud. Hurriedly, I get Kat out, wrapping her up in my arms and carrying her inside.

I lay her down on the same cot that Pawn used when he kept watch over Feather, or, rather, Emily Scott, here. I hold my fingers to her wrists and then neck, looking for a pulse. I can't feel anything. Shit. I can't feel her chest rise or fall either, and the doctor warned me not to touch her. But I do set his equipment up as instructed. My hand goes inside my cut for my pack of smokes and I light one up while pacing the floor. And I wait.

A car door slams outside after what feels like hours, and I meet him at the entrance, holding the door open for him. The doctor quickly begins his exam of Kat's body. He checks her breathing with a stethoscope before attaching pads to her chest under her shirt and flipping a machine on that registers a barely-there heartbeat.

"Hand me the IV I brought. It has meds to help counteract the paralytic she ingested."

Fear laces my veins and I pray that she is alive. I also pray that Tank doesn't kill us all for what we did.

The doctor interrupts my thoughts after checking her over. "She's alive but took a bad hit to the head and may have bruised some ribs in the crash. Give her time to wake up. I'll be back to check on her." He writes a few notes down on a pad of paper before leaving and giving me more instructions.

I pull my phone out and give Blade a call. "Spider," he answers right away.

"She took a hit to the head and has bruised ribs, but she's alive. Where is Tank? He needs to get up here."

"He took off before we could tell him what happened, and his phone is off. I can't call him. The boys are out now looking for him."

An exhausted breath escapes me. "Fuck."

"Yeah, fuck. Keep her alive and keep me posted." He hangs up and my hand drops to my side.

When will this shit ever end? Something tells me it's about to get worse yet before it starts getting better.

Kat

A painful gasp startles me awake, and I start choking on air. My ribs feel like shattered glass. I hold my chest trying to compress them while my body refuses to stop coughing. Keeping myself tight, I roll over and fall to the floor, with the nausea that hits me turning my stomach. But I can't breathe and keep choking every time I try inhaling. My lungs violently protest the stress from practically being dead. On my hands and knees, I continue coughing and choking until it slowly starts to get better.

Another minute and I am able to take a few calming, deep breaths in. There is water sitting next to the cot and I take gulps of it, holding the glass with one shaky hand as I look around. I'm at the mine. That means we failed, and Matias is alive. Damn it.

It's pitch black in the room except for a small lamp on the desk which lights up a little of the area around it. I push myself up from the floor and my head spins from the movement. My eyes shut and I wince from the massive headache and throbbing pain on the left side of my head. Flashbacks hit me every which way. I see Matias at Tami's house and then punching me in the car.

I set the water down and hold my throbbing temples for a moment before I go in search of Tank. He can't be too far.

As soon as I step outside the front door, a whisper of smoke catches my attention.

"You look pretty alive for a dead girl."

"Spider, where is Tank? And what happened?"

"Don't know." He pulls in a long drag and I wait until he exhales. "Tank lost his shit. He shot at the SUV and it crashed with you inside. I don't think he realized you were in there. He took off before we could explain to him that you were alive. I can't track him down."

Holy shit, this is bad. This game is a fucking mess.

"How can you guys *not* be able to find him? I *told* you all that waiting for Matias was a bad idea, that it wouldn't work." My hands run over my face and through my long hair. "Get me out of here. I have to go find him. How long was I out?"

Spider tosses his smoke in the dirt and turns toward me. "You've been out for two days. You think you can find him, Kat? We've been looking for him and haven't had any luck, but *you* can?"

"Spider, you are looking for him in all the wrong the places. You are looking where he would go. When, I guarantee you, he's looking for me."

"That makes no goddamn sense, Kat. He thinks you are dead."

"Yeah, until he figures this all out or he goes after Matias alone, Spider." That, and he had to have found the thumb drive, I just know it. He's a whole day ahead of us. "He's going to fucking die in Mexico if I don't get to him first." I start pacing. "I need to leave and go after him."

"How the hell are you going to get over the border?"

"I'm not going over the border. Matias isn't leaving the States until he gets what he came for. Me. The only way to save us all is to kill Matias. He believes I'm dead, like we wanted. Now I can hunt him down and he'll never see it coming."

I was never supposed to make it back here so quickly. Matias was supposed to take me, but not in front of Tami. I steered clear from her, but he had known how to draw me out. I was going to kill him in his sleep after I woke up. The car crash messed everything up and now Tank is missing.

"Let's go then, but it stays the same. No one is to know you are alive." I couldn't agree more, so I nod my head in the dark.

Spider takes me into Reno. He thinks he's coming with me but he's not. I don't work with anyone and I'll be faster on my own.

We stop at a gas station and he fills up his truck. I look around and spot a mom in a van with California plates. She picks up the toddler from the seat behind her and walks inside.

Quietly and slowly, I get out from the truck and creep around the pump, only to find Spider standing on the other side. His deep scowl startles me as he advances forward until we are nose to nose. "Are you Tank's woman or not?"

I scowl back, "Don't fuck with me, Spider."

"Get your ass in the truck. You are on my watch, Kat. You don't do shit without my say so. You are property of Battle Born, and you are not leaving alone and hurt right now. If something happened to you, Tank would never fuckin' forgive me. Move."

His arms flex with the bite of his voice, and I believe he will make a scene to protect me, for his brother. He also knows that I can't make a scene. Fucker.

Swallowing my pride, I get back into the truck and he finishes filling the tank while keeping his eyes pinned to my location the entire time. He's not the Sergeant-at-Arms for nothing.

He slams his door shut and glares, "Where would Tank go first?"

I hesitate and almost tell him the cabin, but Tank is not there, I know he is not.

"He probably found the thumb drive I left for him which set him on a goose chase of clues that no one else would find but him."

I take a moment to think, and gaze out the window. Spider starts the truck and pulls out of the gas station.

"My guess is that, by now, he's in California looking for the family I asked him to save for me. Next, he'll go to Mexico to kill Matias. We need to stop him."

I say it more for myself than for Spider, and he doesn't say anything back so he must agree that Tank just became a priority in this game of life or death.

CHAPTER 4

Tank

The rumble of another bike rolling up the street steals my attention away from the little boy in the yard. In my mirror, I see a Hispanic biker riding up closer, with a lit cigar hanging from his mouth. What the ever-loving-fuck is happening here? How did he ever find me?

"*Que pasa, pinche pendejo?*" Cuervo smirks while parking his bike alongside mine and looking around. "Nice white neighborhood."

He looks around some more but stalls his movement and removes the cigar from his mouth to point with two fingers, "Aw, but that is no white kid. *Now* I see." He places the cigar back into his mouth and takes a few puffs. "Say something, *pendejo*." He arches his brow high up over his shades, looking irritated.

"How and why are you here?"

"Patched in with the Reno chapter, *cabrón*. As soon as I heard you went nomad, I came to save your ass from being stabbed."

"Why would I be stabbed?"

"Because, *estúpido*, that's all I thought about since I met you." He takes another drag. "We need to move, *ese*. Before those white bitches call the cops on my brown ass for parking on their street. *Entiendes*?"

"*Sí, pendejo.*"

I can't help the grin that creeps up the corner of my mouth when Cuervo's head jerks back in surprise and then scowls from me calling him stupid. I learned a lot from Kat. And, instantly, that thought douses my mood. Cuervo nods his head and hits the gas on his bike, heading up the road. I crank my bike on and follow him deep into the city.

He doesn't stop until he finds a place in town referred to by the locals as Little Tijuana. We park our bikes outside of a bar that's blaring Mariachi music. As soon as we sit down, the waitress brings us two draft beers and shots of tequila. I take in the stares that the bar patrons give me.

Cuervo laughs and shoots his tequila, then takes a long chug of his brew. Where in the fuck did he bring me?

"Hey, *cabrón*," he sets his glass down, "You keep traveling down this road alone, you'll stay that way. The highway becomes a mistress to the life you once knew and loved."

"What exactly are you getting at, Cuervo? I can't go back there and live the life I had made there without her in it. I can't look at the faces that were brothers to me but left me out in the cold. Tell me, old man, how the fuck do you get past that?"

"You fucking don't. You can't replace the love of the woman you loved. *That* will never happen."

My chest heaves and I fight back the pain and emotion from showing in front of this man.

"I used to be you, Tank, *muchos años atrás*, many years ago. All laughs and jokes. Making a lot of *feria*, some fat cash on the side. Until Rosa died. I died with her."

Cuervo lifts a hand up, signaling the waitress, "*Una botella de tequila*," then points at the table. Fairly quickly, a cute young girl delivers a bottle. Cuervo picks it up and pours us shots, then pushes a glass toward me. I take one shot and set the glass down. He patiently waits as I pour and then take another, and then another. When I've caught up to his number, he continues.

"The anger replaced who I was. No more jokes and laughs. That's why I hated you so much, Tank, you were me while she was alive, before I fucked it all up." He takes another shot and refills the empty glasses. "Kat is *mi familia* and belonged to Rosa, and she loved her. Is that her *niño*?" he questions and then points at the bottle.

I shoot the liquid down my throat and allow the burn to mix in with the open hole in my chest. "I think so." I grind my teeth to keep from yelling out my pain.

"What are your plans with the *niño*?"

"Keep him safe from his father and move him."

"Then what?"

I don't know, honestly. I'm living moment to moment and haven't thought past keeping him alive. Cuervo sees the hesitation in my eyes.

"He could stay with the *familia* he has now and could be perfectly safe." My gut sinks at that thought and something that I don't even understand hurts. Some part of me had claimed him, and, until this moment, I didn't see it, that this little boy has hooked me. "*Or*, what would *Kat* want?"

My chest tightens at his words and Cuervo continues on. He rips open a wound I wasn't prepared for. "Maybe it is just me, but he belongs with his *real familia*. He has our blood. One day he'll thirst to know more, and he won't understand himself. Teach him, Tank, take him and be a father to him. You need to choose the road I never did, leave your mistress, and be a father."

He signals the waitress back over and orders us a huge plate of tacos that we eat in silence. It's odd that out of all the brothers who could've come for me, it was Cuervo. I could be wrong, but his words, I would bet my left nut that he's never shared those words with anyone other than his brother, Fuego. A part of me appreciates the crazy bastard just a bit more than I did the day before.

"How are we taking the kid back?" he asks with a sly grin.

CHAPTER 5

Kat

Spider's been hot on my tail and I can't even take a piss without him knowing it. He knows I'm attempting to take off alone to go find Tank, and he is serious about making me Tank's Ol' Lady, literally. I need Tank back ASAP. I can't live like this.

"Spider," I call from across the motel room. "Do Vegas and the girls think I died?"

"Yes." He watches me closely. "Why? You don't want them to hate you when they find out you are alive?" He grins at his own snarky comment.

God, he's a prick. "If they do, I can't blame them. I can deal with it," I bite back.

"Kat, you are going to learn what a family is at some point. They aren't going to hate you." He snickers, "They sure did rub off on you though. I don't think I've ever heard you talk so much, and here I thought you were one of the guys."

"Asshole," I glare at his gloating face. "*You* should talk. You are always in everyone's business more than you should be, and don't deny it."

We stare each other down, waiting for the other one to break. After a few seconds, I realize that we have bigger problems to deal with, so I snatch my clothes that Spider had brought for me off the bed.

I need a shower before we hit the road to go after Tank, and I have a new partner. Yay me. Slamming the door behind me, I hear Spider mutter, "Bitch". God, he's like the little brother I never wanted to tag along. My hands aggressively push the pants off my legs, and, when I grip my top to tear it away, my ribs protest with an intense pain.

My breath is stolen away from me and I let go of the shirt instantly. My hands start shaking and my eyes water. I slow down and gradually lift it up to find a large bruise on my left side. Somehow, my ribs were damaged, probably from the car accident. My fingertips gently graze over the purple and blue skin before I am brave enough to lift the shirt again. With more caution, I attempt it again and slowly remove it without lifting my arm very far.

After my clothes are off, I stand still and stare at my face in the mirror. The monster bruise on my temple is a reminder of what happened. Matias, I can't even say husband because he's not that, he tried to kill me with a single blow to my head. The bruising ghosts over my eye and the side of my face, showing the brutal mark of a killer. Memories of the past creep in like an old friend. Of the man who raped and beat me for years.

The abuse I wear on my face now is the same one that I wore on my heart for years. If I could go back, I would shoot the cold bastard when he was lying next to me. Never again will I be the woman I once was. I'm stronger, and there is no room for the past anymore. He doesn't hold my heart in his hands anymore, Tank does.

The hot water relaxes my sore muscles and I take a moment to clean up before I feel strong enough to fight again. I'm ready to go find my Ol' Man. I want his brand. I want it all. And I want my baby back with me.

As quickly as possible, I put clothes on and braid my hair before meeting Spider back in the room.

Cold as ice, I hold my hand out and Spider observes me before handing over a gun and then a knife. "Welcome back."

"We are taking the Tesla," I inform him.

"The fucking *what*? How much money do you *have*, woman?"

I don't answer but the squint in my amused eyes says a-fucking-lot.

Spider drives us to the storage shed and I'm happy to find what I do inside. An open laptop and a mess. Only Tank would leave it this way and my computer on. God, that man! How can someone so smart be so dense? I log off and Spider's face is priceless.

"He didn't actually get into your computer, did he?"

"Obviously did."

"Holy shit."

I can read the questions circling behind those eyes, and, had he asked, I would've told him what he wanted to know, for the most part. I'm done hiding. It's time to end it all, and I have never felt freer. "Let's go. I'll pull the car out and you can park your truck in here."

"Give me your laptop, I don't want you taking off on me."

A sinister smile plasters on my face and I toss the computer in the air. Spider almost drops it and cradles it like gold to his chest. Idiot. He gets into my car after he parks the truck and locks the storage shed. He drives us onto the freeway, heading toward California. Maybe it's not so bad to have him around. I still feel a little dizzy and exhausted after everything.

I just pray that Tank went to get exactly what I asked him to. My baby. Eli.

Hours pass and Spider stays focused on the road in front of him. He whistles low, "You already knew everything, Kat. You came in stacked."

"Made my life easy, I knew where to look already," I shrug a shoulder.

Spider finally cracked during the long drive, and asked a few questions. Most he already knew the answers to. I have no doubt that Tank does as well, and I have never felt better. I just hope that he still wants me, the way I am, and with the things I have done. Will he understand? I do know that I will fight for him, and us.

Slowly, we crawl up the street that the Hoffmans live on with my son, and my blood pressure spikes. My hands touch the window and Spider slows down and parks the car behind another, a few houses down.

"No," my voice cracks. "How did he find them?"

Through the tinted windows of my car, we watch Matias' men scour the property and take out a few things to their car.

"Shit, Spider, I don't think Tank got here in time. What if Matias took Tank too?" My breathing picks up and panic sets in at the sight of the black suits in the house that protected my son for his entire life.

Wetness hits my cheeks and rolls down, falling onto my heaving chest. Silently, I hurt. In this moment, I want to die more than I want to live. If they have taken them, it will be near impossible to find Eli. Matias would hide him far better than I ever could. The sting of the truth is brutal. I have failed him, my Eli.

My fingers roam over the waistband of my pants. All I need is to make them hurt, like me. I want them full of bullets for touching something that was so sacred to me.

"Kat!" Spider whisper shouts. I snap out of the trance I was overtaken by, a vision of blood and death. "We don't know that they took either of them."

"Get Tank on the phone then," I snarl. "Have him tell me where my baby is."

My head snaps away from Spider and I can hear him on the phone with Blade who confirms that they found Tank's phone in our house. There is no way to contact him, and now Cuervo is missing, too. They haven't told Emilia yet.

Red. I see red. Enough already. It's time they all died. Matias' empire will fall by my hand.

"They all are going to die. *El día de los Muertos.*"

"Kat, we need to go back to Reno. We can't stay here alone, with no backup."

"Fucking leave then, Spider. I am not owned by the club."

"Yes, you are."

My face tears up and I turn to him. "Really? Where is the brand on my body?" God, I wish I would have gotten it when I had the chance.

"Brand or fucking not, you belong to us and Tank." Spider's face grows dark. "Don't make me tell you again."

"I'm killing these assholes before I go back to Reno. You can help me or leave me here. I will find a way. No one touches what is mine."

"After we confirm Tank and the kid are not with them."

I could argue with Spider that they aren't because they would be riding with Matias who doesn't stick around for the clean-up. The time we wait for them has given us the chance to come up with a plan, then we sit and wait. The two SUV's pull out of the driveway at dusk.

From under the back seat, I pull out a large case and open it to get out a sniper's rifle. I check the chamber and clip to ensure they are loaded. Snapping everything into place, I open the maps on my phone, unsure of where they may go.

"We need to get them on the first turn, about two miles up the road. There is a drop-off. Stay about two hundred yards back so I can make the first shot."

"You can hit a moving target at that distance?"

My glare could kill Spider for doubting me. "I will hit my target," my jaw clenches.

Spider follows back as instructed. I crawl into the back seat and open the sunroof. As the turn approaches, I stand. One long breath goes in and the wind drags me back. I hold the rifle steady and my finger holds the trigger with steady pressure. When the first SUV hits the turn, I pull the trigger and send a bullet through the front right tire. The SUV swerves and rolls over the railing, down the steep embankment.

The second driver slams on his breaks, and I wait for it to stop. "Pull over!" I yell at Spider when I lower myself back down into the car. He parks at an angle and I jump out to take aim from the dirt on the side of the car. When two men get out, I send a bullet to the front tire and then through the heart of one of them. The guy standing next to him foolishly draws his handgun out.

Not wasting time, I shoot him in the heart as well. My next shot is the gas tank. I hit it and light the sky up. But, that's not enough, and I send more shots. It's still not enough. I need more of them to die. The agony is too much.

A soft hand lands on my shoulder and I snap out of it. My cheeks are drenched with the tears that I didn't even realize I had. "Time to go."

I hand him my rifle and stand up, wiping my face, then dusting my pants off.

What have I done? It doesn't matter because I will not stop until I make everyone hurt. After all I have gone through, even changing Eli's birth certificate to hide him, I still lost him. Matias found him.

I wear the tattoo of black wings of an angel on my back and arms. These tattoos represent my flight into hell.

I'm taking the devil with me.

CHAPTER 6

Kat

Spider and I made it back to Reno a few days ago. No one knows where Tank is, or Cuervo for that matter who doesn't care to carry a cell phone with him. Everyone has been going nuts trying to locate the two of them. I've been scouring the internet, and not being able to call favors in has crippled me. I'm not sure that Matias knows who the Black Widow is. But, if he does, he would know I was alive as soon as I contacted anyone.

I sit in this dump of an apartment that I found to hide in for now. Still not able to get a location on Matias to find Eli. Nothing. All leads have dried up. I have to start over. No one will talk to me without knowing who I am.

I look out the window and watch cars and people pass by. Wishing I had the easy life. But all I can focus on is the pain. The only thing I know to be real and tangible.

A loud, mouthy woman comes barreling down the building's hallway. What the hell is going on?

"Open the motherfucking door, Kat!" Vegas booms from the other side, her fist slamming against the door.

"Vegas, shut the hell up and go home," Spider snarls at her.

I can't feel much, the numbness and pain having shattered me, but I do sluggishly get up to open the door. What do I have to lose at this point? My hand goes to the mediocre locks and the door swings open, almost hitting me in the process. Vegas flings her body at me and wraps her arms around my neck.

Her grip is so fierce that she's choking me and causing me to wince. Over her shoulder, I see Jenn and Dana standing back with hurt expressions. I step out of Vegas' death grip to walk back over to my seat at the window.

"I don't know what the hell has been going on with you, but start at the beginning. And then I will kick your ass for killing us with your fake death." Vegas demands answers and settles in. She takes a seat in front of me while Dana and Jenn pull the table chairs up. Spider huffs and shuts the door, stepping out, but he has the phone to his ear telling Blade what his wife has done. That she followed him to my location.

Not bothering to care about the secrets anymore, I start from the beginning and tell them all the details. Who my father is and about the death of my mother. The intense training he made me do and the people he made me kill at a very young age. I retell the stories of Matias and his abuse. I don't leave out any detail.

When I get to Eli, I smile through the tears when I tell them about his birth. How I held him in my arms and memorized his perfect face before leaving him with the Hoffmans.

I confess all my sins to my sisters in hopes that they find forgiveness in their hearts for me. Everyone leaves me eventually. But a part of me is resigned to my fate of being alone and dead inside. They can have it all and see me bare.

At some point, Spider comes back into the room. His face is stoic, but he has gentle eyes. I don't want his pity, so I look away.

The room is cloaked in silence when I get to the end. The part where I failed, and I lost the two most important people to me. I want to feel again, but I can only feel the gut-wrenching agony.

"What have I done?" I plead. "I lost them." Forgiveness or not, this will not return them to me.

Jenn, the strongest of them all, doesn't look at me with sadness but with understanding. She sees that, until I right my world, I won't survive. If they died, I die.

"Kat, I am here to help you kill the demons that haunt you," she simply states, "However that is, I will do that for you."

Vegas nods and agrees, "I am in. No one fucks with my bitches and gets away with it."

Dana starts and stops before she says what is eating at her. "Kat, what you must have felt when you held each of our babies—" She swallows past the lump in her throat. "God, I just, I— am..." She clears her throat. "I will help you however I can for you to get back at that asshole."

I know she wanted to say she was sorry for it all. But it is not their fault.

"I just need to find him and end it already. Until then, I will keep searching. I will never give up until he is dead."

After that, the girls and I sit and drink vodka, the silence a comfortable friend. Not much can be said, but their support means everything to me. They didn't know the answers and yet, they trusted me. A rare gift of respect and faith.

"How is Tami?" I absently ask. "Cash?"

Jenn looks a little ashen. "I think we need to tell her about you being alive. She's taken it pretty hard, Kat. She was the closest to you."

I really do feel horrible about what she had to have gone through. I wanted to keep her safe and protected but I couldn't do that fully, and I hate that I couldn't.

"We can't tell her until it's over. If I do die, I don't want her to go through this again. I may not make it out of this alive."

Vegas nods like a boss. "I agree, she may also slip and say something on accident, not realizing she tipped something off." I've missed these girls. It feels better somehow to have them sit here to share my problems with.

Dana, always the fixer and more than not the sober one of us all, comes up with an idea. "Matias is lying under the radar, right?"

All heads turn to look at her in interest. "He hasn't been home yet. What would be the biggest distraction of all to get him out of hiding again?" She hesitates because not one of us can answer so she continues. "If he does have the baby, and that is a big if, Kat, because we haven't confirmed that, would your being alive be able to be used to bargain with money and contacts, to get your son back?" she grins an evil gleam.

Vegas and Jenn join in her enthusiasm, and it hits me. "Do you think that Tank could be hiding Eli? Why he and Cuervo have gone off the grid completely? Why hasn't Matias gone home yet?" My thoughts run wild, almost afraid to hope. God, I feel hope that I haven't had in days.

Dana beams with pride, "Could be that, too. No one could kidnap Tank. He's like a big ass kid no one wants to take, even to kill, you know what I am saying?"

"Hell yeah, I do. I couldn't get him away from me fast enough."

Vegas laughs, "If anyone could get to your baby in time, it would be that man. He lives to be the glorified hero. He's waiting for a big entrance and to make it dramatic, I bet."

My head starts to spin, finally awake with whispering of promises. Could I still save it all *and* myself?

Spider walks into the bathroom and I pull the girls in quick to help me create a distraction to get out of here alone and without him on my tail. Jenn turns up the music and the rest of the girls spread throughout the apartment. Vegas tosses me her keys and I'm out the door in seconds.

CHAPTER 7

Tank

Jane Hoffman is one little mean momma bear.

"I don't know you, and Katherine never told me anything about you." She stands guard, with her hands on her hips, and stares me down through the screen door that is between us.

"Jane," I take a brief moment to count to three in my head before I start screaming at this tiny woman. "Kat is not in a position to tell you herself. Can I please come in and explain myself better?"

"No, you cannot, Mr...?" she raises a brow at me.

"Lucas Taylor, Mrs. Hoffman."

Cuervo snickers from behind me and she scowls at him, glancing around me.

"This is Cuervo, he is Katherine's uncle." And I hope that gives me some reassurance with this woman.

"Jane," a man calls from the back of the house. Eventually, he finds the three of us at the front door. He is carrying the little boy with him who, when he notices Jane, he wiggles out of his hold and calls for her by her name. She takes him from her husband's arms and kisses his cheek.

"These are Lucas and Cuervo, here to talk about Katherine." She bounces the small boy on her hip, and he chuckles along with her down the hallway.

"Mr. Hoffman," I begin again, "I need to talk to you about Katherine. It's very important and urgent, if you could give us a few moments?"

He steps through the screen door and shakes mine and then Cuervo's hand. "Danny Hoffman."

On his forearm, I notice a tattoo that's customary for a street kid. He knows the criminal world and knows it well having been involved, at some point in his life, with one of the biggest gangs in the L.A. area.

"Why are you two here?" he asks and points to the chairs on the front porch. The three of us take a seat. I want to start but I can't make myself to say the words out loud.

Cuervo jumps in, "Katherine's husband found her. She has passed." Danny's shocked face turns away from him to meet my eyes. I look away, unable to show him the pain and truth that lay in Cuervo's words.

Finding some courage, I take over the conversation. "We have reason to believe her husband could be on his way here. We tracked down the man who had forged the papers for her son," I point to the house. "The man turned up dead just before Matias attacked Katherine in Reno. We think that he was going to get Katherine first, then the kid. He needed her to get to him. You are not safe here. Eventually, he *will* find you."

Danny takes a moment and sits back in his chair, looking at the both of us before making his decision.

"Where are we headed to?"

Jane is less than happy with the abrupt departure from their home when her husband explains the situation to her. However, she is willing to do it for Eli.

That is Kat's son's name, and I can't seem to tear my eyes away from the little boy who looks so much like his mother.

"Only pack what you can't live without for twenty-four hours. We can buy the rest. Leave everything as normal as possible," I advise her because she looks as if she wants to pack the entire house. "They will come here looking. They will walk through the house, and we want them to think that you are only out for the day."

She really glares at us when her husband takes their cell phones and hands them over to me to turn off. I feel bad for her because she's probably never seen real danger from this kind of people. We are taking her out of her home. Maybe, at some point, she will see that having her life and future is better than having a house.

You can always make a new home with those you love when you have them around.

Eli is a great kid. He slept and played the whole way back to Reno. We took the congested freeways through California and gave him as many breaks as he needed. Cuervo and I took turns driving the Hoffmans' van back. We stored our bikes with a family friend that Cuervo had at a sister chapter.

My life was wrapped up in that bike. I had never left it in the care of another person before. I bought her down in Vegas and rode her for good luck down the strip with Stryker, Mad Max, Blade and all of us. It was a blow to my nuts to throw a sheet over her as I thought of all the miles and memories made with my club while riding it.

But, for Eli, I would sell it. For Kat, I would blow it to hell and back.

There is something missing and I can't quite figure out what it is yet. Time on the road is where I do most of my thinking. I would normally lean on my brothers for guidance. I feel stripped down to the core. If I do rebuild the man that is left of me, I am not sure what I will find or be. But a whole new life awaits me.

I think about these things and it pisses me off that I don't feel like I could call Axl or Blade to talk to them about this shit. So, I take Eli to the safest place I could think of, mine and Kat's cabin.

Cuervo called Emilia from one of our random stops. He used payphones. I had no idea they had those around still, but he found them. He gave her a grocery list and the location where to meet us. Emilia did everything without question, a true Ol' Lady, and all that did was tear my damn bleeding heart out.

We loaded the van up, and now, here I sit, watching Eli as he's trying to chase some small birds in the back yard. His joy and laughter sound like a sad song, a broken melody to my ears.

While Jane and Danny argue over what's next, I already know what is going to happen. They are going to get lost for a while and leave Eli here with me.

Emilia is watching the same show as me, and a tear runs down her cheek. She sees Kat in him, too. She runs a hand over my back, "It will be okay, *mijo*. He's such a beautiful *niño*, *sí*?"

"Yeah," my voice cracks, unable to elaborate any further.

The voices from inside the cabin get louder and I have finally lost my patience. I storm in, ready to set them straight.

"Look, Jane, I get that you have been Eli's mother for all intents and purposes, and you've been looking after him since he was a baby. I *get* that." My eyes meet her surprised ones. "But he belongs with me now. You will be in constant danger because of who he *is*. Also, he is *my* responsibility because I loved his mother. She was *mine*."

"Tank."

I freeze and the air from my lungs vanishes. Jane and Danny are both staring in astonishment in the direction the voice from the heavens came from.

"Tank," the dark angel calls my name again. I run my hands over my face just before feeling a tender touch on my back. Instantly, my knees buckle with the weight of the situation, and I feel like I'm losing my damn mind. This can't be right.

"Baby," she cries, and I hold my face in my hands, on my knees, not wanting to look up and realize that she's not really here. Small hands grip my wrists. "It's me, Tank, please look at me?" She lightly pulls my hands down, and she *is* here when I open my eyes. She, too, is kneeling in front of me, with smeared mascara running down her cheeks.

My hands shake before they hold her face and my thumbs wipe the pain away with the moisture. She closes her eyes and tilts her head back, whispering, "I didn't think I would get to feel your touch again, and I was haunted by the memory of you."

I pull her to me, and my lips savagely take hers in a kiss. A resurrection of her and also reassurance that she really is here in front of me and this is not a dream.

My tongue pushes inside her mouth and searches for more, claiming more. She opens and draws me into her. The craving is extraordinary as we devour the other and share our souls in this kiss.

My teeth trace her bottom lip before I rasp, "If this is a dream or I am dead, I never want to wake up. I want to stay right here with you." My lips press against her swollen ones and I whisper against them, "I love you, K-love."

A shuddering breath is released from Kat, and she barely whispers back the words that have been haunting me. "I love you, Tank."

Nothing can be heard but the sound of our hearts beating, coming back to life and coming alive after thinking the other was gone. I pull back just enough to see her for myself.

Her eyes bat open, and I see where a large bruise marks her face, and the bags under her eyes. I place a kiss over it all and mark it as mine. Kat loses control and falls into my arms sobbing, "I thought I lost you. I thought you had died."

"No, Kat, I've been busy chasing ghosts." A faint smile graces my face. My hand runs over her back, "It's time for you to do something else now, no more of this badass business."

"What?" she looks up at me in confusion.

"Come with me outside. I have someone you need to see."

CHAPTER 8

Kat

Tank stands and leads me to the back door. I feel like my feet are floating as I walk behind him. At first, I hear a small voice squealing, and then I see him. A tiny little human throwing leaves and sticks before falling back and landing on his little baby, diaper padded butt.

My hand grips Tank's like a lifeline, and I can't let go. I am terrified to get close to Eli. What if he cries? What of he hates me? I haven't seen him or been in the same room as him since the day he was born, and that makes me feel so inadequate to be standing in front of him as his mother.

Literally, I am scared to move a muscle, and I stare, feeling mesmerized by his presence while I follow his every move from a short distance.

"Go to him, K-Love, go meet your son," Tank nods his head in Eli's direction.

Tentatively, I take one step and then another until I shuffle my feet along through the dirt, twigs and leaves. Eli's happy laughter gives me a little confidence that it will be okay. I sit down a few feet in front of him and cross my legs.

He turns and squeals, then comes running for me with a little toothy smile and drool rolling down his chin. Wanting to play, his enthusiasm to greet me, to meet an unknown new friend, is contagious. He lunges for me when he's close enough to wrap those little chubby arms around my head, and smears his drool over my face in an open mouthed kiss.

I break.

He doesn't know I am his mother, and why would he?

My hands instinctively hold onto all my hopes and dreams in this little package. I breathe in deep just to smell him again. My baby is in my arms. I laugh with him and I cry like I haven't in years. I fall over to play along with him, pretending that he pushed me over.

"Up," he taps my face and I stand and toss him into the air, smiling while he shouts. When his little body comes back down, I cradle him to my chest and kiss the top of his head. I catch Tank watching us intently and I walk over to him, holding Eli on my hip.

"Tank, this is Eli *Lucas* Taylor."

Tank's big toothy smile meets me this time, "Really? You named him Lucas?" His smile gets a little wider when he hears Eli's middle name is his own first name.

"Hey there, little Lucas, I'm big Lucas. I think you are gonna be Junior from now on, my little mini me. Your mom is a lot crazy, though. Don't worry, she's not allowed to play with her toys anymore. Her job is gonna be to be a momma from now on."

I choke on the words that lodge in my throat. I can't be *just* a mom yet. There is still the huge problem we have with Matias.

"Don't," Tank scolds me, "Protecting this family is *my* job."

My mouth opens to argue but I notice Emilia standing to the side, next to Cuervo, Jane and Danny. All of them look as confused as I am at how it all got so twisted.

Cuervo is the first to break and walks to me with Emilia on his heels to give me a hug. "I'm so glad that we were wrong, *mija*."

Emilia's hands tremble when she reaches out to me. "You better never scare me like you did, ever again." She pushes my hair back behind my ear. "You need some family time, so I am going to take Cuervo home. Call me tomorrow, yes?"

"I will try. I don't know for sure if I can."

She nods in understanding, and they both take off together, leaving us with the Hoffmans. Jane's face is filled with an ache that I know well.

I hand Eli over to Tank and he eagerly jumps into his arms, tugging on Tank's short beard. I step back and let them play, then turn around to approach Jane. "I see your pain and I am sorry that I caused it. I needed your help, and now you are suffering because of giving me your help. I am sorry for that."

Jane looks up at me. "I always knew you were coming back, Katherine. That's why I never had him call me 'mom'. But I can't lie. I will miss him terribly."

"I don't want you to leave. Eli knows and trusts you. Until we have things taken care of, I want you to stay close by. Then, after the dust settles, it will be your decision how much you want to be in his life."

"What needs to be taken care of?" Jane's tone comes off irritated and disapproving. Danny places a hand on her shoulder, "Jane, it's none of our business. We did this to help her, not fix their problems."

I think Danny understands exactly what we are talking about and looks the other way, knowing some evil needs to be destroyed. Also, I can't fault her for feeling protective of Eli. After all, I am the one who put her in that position.

"Can you help me with him to adjust? He will miss you both, too."

She agrees and I think that is as much as I can hope for right now. But she does seem to come around just a little when she suggests, "Let's make dinner and we can discuss how to work this out and his routines." She leads the way and I walk inside behind her. Together, we make dinner and talk more about the future with Eli.

From the kitchen window, I see Tank and Danny chatting as they watch Eli and play with him. It strikes me how much Tank, once again, just takes him and naturally adjusts to whatever situation he's in.

After dinner is done and Eli is asleep in one of the smaller rooms, I lean against the wall and watch him from a short distance. The creak of a board behind me alerts me that Tank is approaching, and, soon, his arms wrap around my waist.

"I need you, Kat."

His nose runs up my neck and fingers trail under my shirt, up to my breasts. He tugs me back against his chest, holding tight with one arm, and I moan when he twists my nipples with his free hand.

My feet drag along the floor with every step he takes backward, stealing me away to our room. He quietly shuts the door and locks it.

"We have a lot to talk about, and I'm mad as hell at you right now. You promised me everything and you lied to me, Kat."

"I didn't lie to you, Tank." I tremble in his arms from the tight grip he has on me. His fingers dig into my stomach and it sends exciting chills through my body. I get high from his commanding nature.

"Really?" he quietly growls. "You promised me *you*, all of you, and you didn't tell me your plans. Who do you belong to, Kat?" He whips me around to face him and leans in, close to my face. "I will never go through *that* again. You and the brothers fucked with my head. That shit tore me apart."

He steps forward, forcing me to back up with how close he is, barreling into my body.

"You either belong to me and I am your priority in your life, along with that little boy, or killing Matias is. Choose, Kat, us or him."

Fury like I've never felt before lights up my temper and I jab a finger in his chest. "It is not fair of you to say that to me. You knew I wasn't telling anyone anything until I could."

We are whisper yelling at each other, careful not to wake anyone in the cabin.

"Oh, so when you *died*, it was safe *then* to tell me what you were doing when Blade and Spider already *knew*?"

"You knew I was going to kill him to save Eli! Don't deny it!"

"A heads-up that you were going to fake kill yourself would have been great. Also, *not* fake kill yourself and let your man handle the man shit, Kat. If you die, then who is going to care for him? Who is going to take care of *me*?"

For a brief moment, we both stop, stunned, and stare at each other, the frustration and pain so high that neither one of us saw the emotion that would collide with our reality. Fighting over the past and who is wrong and who is right.

"You promised me *you*," he growls again at me.

"You have *me*," I growl back.

Tank's hand comes up to wrap around the back of my hair. "Shut up and show me then." He tugs my head back with a quick snap.

My hands find his belt and I slowly unbuckle it while I stare into his eyes. We are so close but so far away. I am sorry that he was hurt. Tank was never to believe that I had died. Through my gaze, I try to show him my devotion. His face is still the Tank that captured my heart, but, something inside him snapped while I was away. I broke him and us.

My chest heaves as I try to hide the disappointment I feel at that thought. My lip trembles and my mouth slightly opens as I try to take small amounts of air into my lungs. I fumble with the zipper and he stops me with a hand over mine, halting my progress.

His eyes dart between both of mine, and I break. I feel too fragile to fight with Tank. He has the power to destroy me. This is worse than believing he died.

He patiently waits for me. I can't take the pressure and I try to pull away from his grip and run. He tightens his grip even more. "Stop fucking running from me."

A single tear rolls down my cheek and he leans forward to lick it away. "If you are mine, you will surrender your heart and body to me. You will let me take care of you. Come to me for strength, Kat. It's what I know you need. But you need to learn to trust. Get naked and kneel on the bed."

His deep baritone sends shivers up my spine and I do as he asks. I strip all the clothes from my body and Tank removes his t-shirt just as I kneel before him on the bed. The height of the bed brings me higher than standing on my own and closer to his own height.

Tank pulls the belt from his pants, leaving the zipper open. "Kat," he calmly calls me to him, and my eyes go up to meet his stern ones. "You need to release your pain and stress, and you want pain to do that?"

I choke on the harsh reality of what I need, and Tank sees it. Had my life been that messed up that I need that now?

"Don't," he commands. "It's what you need and crave, and I crave to give it to you. Trust me."

"I trust you," I say on a faint whisper.

"Tell me what you need," he raises a brow at me.

"I need you to make it hurt." He waits for me to continue. "I want you to touch me." Still, he waits for me to keep going. "Tank, I'm tired and I need your strength. I am terrified I broke you and us."

He tilts his head, pleased with my words that were almost impossible for me to confess. Tank stands in front of me and runs a finger across my jaw. "It takes a lot to break me. The pieces will heal with time, but I do need something from you."

"What?"

"Your submission. All of you belongs to me, every aspect of your life. You need something, you come to me. Most importantly, no more secrets." He leans forward and kisses the corner of my mouth. "When I give it to you soft and slow, it is for me, and you want that because you know it is me worshipping you."

"Okay," I squeak out, feeling exposed and raw.

"Good. Let me give you what you need first." Another soft kiss before he stands up straight. "Turn around and ass up."

Doing as he asked, I arch my back on my hands and knees. His finger trails down my back to my pussy and then clit. He rubs me slowly as he admits, "I cannot live without you, K-Love. I need you just as much." He rubs me softly and tenderly, working me up until I squirm, needing more from him.

He pinches my clit and I gasp. "You ready for more?"

"Yes," I hiss.

"Put your hands in front of you and don't move them until I tell you to."

Eagerly, I place my hands above my head and spread my legs farther apart. Tank chuckles and lays a quick smack across my ass cheek. The belt, he runs it across my bare ass. "Let me know if you need more or less."

The belt is gone and then a loud thwack echoes across the room before the bite of the leather registers. I moan out loud and he runs his hands over my ass and kisses the mark left behind.

"More," I beg him.

He gives me four more quick whips with his belt and my hands beg to be released. They clench and pull at the blanket underneath me. My pussy throbs with a delicious desire to stroke it for release.

Tank kisses down my back and kneels behind me as he kisses the marks he made. His lips cool and caress the burn on my heated flesh.

"This is fucking beautiful, baby." He takes one long lick from my clit to my pussy lips, groans and laps at me before going back to my clit.

His tongue goes to work and licks quick and hard, and I'm off in seconds as I'm coming for him. Tank doesn't stop and it is complete torture that he doesn't, but also heaven.

My body relaxes into his touch, and I let him have what he wants. I submit for him. I feel him stopping for a moment, and I can swear that he's smiling. I smile with him in the dark. He goes back to work, licking my pussy. I moan as I get there again and my stomach starts clenching.

Tank's thumb goes into my pussy before he rubs around the tight muscles of my asshole. My body tenses because that has never happened to me. Before I can protest or think to, he slowly sinks in and continues sucking at my clit. The pleasure from him playing with my asshole is unexpected, and I push back into his hand.

He picks up the pace and I pant out loud, moaning and begging him not to stop. "Make me come, Tank. Fuck, don't stop." There is no stopping the build-up that comes when I explode from coming with his thumb in my ass. I fucking love it.

After my body stops contracting, Tank places a kiss over my pussy and stands to remove his pants. When I turn around, he's naked and his dick is steel in front of me. I crawl forward and take his long, thick length in my hand, stroking it softly. The whole meaning of taking it soft and slow hits home in my head.

Bending forward, I take him sweetly in my mouth and bob up and down. I worship him and his body like he said he would do to me. I take my time and bring him to the brink of coming down my throat.

He pulls me up to him and his mouth devours mine in a hungry kiss, full of love. I open for him and honor him back. He tosses me back suddenly, and I laugh when he covers my body with his. Slowly, he lifts my leg and enters me, moving with a steady rhythm, enjoying the feel of our connection.

"Rub that clit, K-Love."

I wet my finger in his mouth and stroke circles over my clit. He picks up my other leg and hammers his cock into me.

"Fuck me, baby, come inside me. Claim us again."

Tank does. We come undone. Together.

CHAPTER 9

Tank

Kat's warm body is snuggled into mine and I wouldn't move for anything, except that my stomach is growling and I am starving for breakfast. Her hand runs up from my stomach to my chest as she starts to wake up. Instantly, I am hard and hungry for something else.

A little cry from Eli fills the air from the other room. Kat sits up straight, startled by the noise and jolts out of bed, tossing a t-shirt over her head and pulling her pants on. She grabs her gun, ready to kill any person who could possibly be threatening her son.

Just as fast, I am up, and my hand is over the gun she's holding. At the same time, we hear Jane settling Eli down and cooing at him, telling him to come eat.

"K-Love, I think he's okay. Finish getting dressed and go out there with them."

She looks a little confused and ashamed at the same time. She puts her long hair up in a messy bun, then slips her bra on. Before stepping out, she looks back and asks, "Are you not coming?"

"Yeah, after a cold shower. I was ready for you."

Kat's gaze flicks down to my rock-hard dick and back up to my face. A smirk covers her face because

I'm still butt ass naked from last night. "You're going to need an ice-cold shower." She leaves me alone with no remorse in her tone whatsoever.

"And a fucking hand to take care of it," I mock out loud to no one but myself.

After a quick a shower, I find Kat at the table with a sad face. I look around and realize why. It is ten in the morning. We slept in while Jane and Danny were up taking care of Eli. He was crying for a snack, breakfast was long gone and he was all cleaned up.

I pretend that I don't see it and start on some scrambled eggs for us. Kat makes Eli a quesadilla and cuts it into little triangles, and she tries damn hard not to let the disappointment shine through. This little boy breaks her down like no one else on this earth could.

It hits home to me that everything she held so close was for him. I can't blame her for the things she did. More than likely, had I been in her situation, I would have done the same.

Taking our plates and coffee to the table, I pass one of each to Kat and kiss her temple. She looks down at the food and then to me, and moisture coats her eyes. Rapidly, she blinks away the tears and concentrates on eating. My hand rubs her back in long slow strokes. Her lungs take in a long inhale and then a slow exhale, releasing the emotion with it. Her heart's basic needs have been ignored for so long. Has she ever had someone to show her love and care? I doubt it very much.

Eli's anxious little hands reach for my eggs. "Bro," I laugh at him, "Noted. Never make food for just two. It is two-point-five people. Just so you know," I explain while giving him some of my eggs, "I don't like to share. But you're a growing boy, so I'll share with you." I wink at him before swiping a piece of the quesadilla off his plate.

Kat's body slightly chuckles next to me. "What, it's what families do, share." She freezes on the spot. "Momma," I kiss her forehead and sit back. A stunned woman blinks back at me. Apparently, love is the best way to shut this woman up. Huh, I'm filing this tidbit away for later.

"Momma," Eli repeats after me several times. This time, Kat is unable to hold back from hiding herself away. She puts her hands over her face and tries her damnedest to control herself.

"K-Love," I call to her, "A mother does what is right for her baby. You *did* that." She shutters a breath out and looks up at me. "You are his momma. Yeah, we slept in today because we didn't think ahead because we never had to before. Like everything else, you will kick ass at this, and we will figure the rest out together."

I glance to the side and Jane gives me an approving nod from where she's standing by the kitchen sink, right before Eli ruins my moment of pure greatness.

"Ass," he parrots and Jane's eyebrows hit her hairline.

I glare at him, "We need to talk about the words you repeat after me. Of all the things I just said, Junior, that's what you pick to repeat? Low, little dude, really low." I shake my head at him, and he throws his scrambled eggs at my chest. "Don't waste food, Eli," I reprimand. He does it again.

"I see we are going to need a lot of team building here." I pick up a piece of egg from my shirt and pop it into my mouth.

Jane chuckles on her way out, and I whisper to Kat, "Lil' momma, he's been living with those missionaries for too long. He throws food!"

Together, her and I clean up the mess and take Eli for a short hike to a lake nearby, for a picnic. There is a trail leading from the cabin and winding through the trees. With a backpack full of sandwiches and drinks, I follow behind the two of them. After about five minutes, Eli starts to run out of steam and slows down.

"Come here, *bebé*," Kat holds her hands out and he runs to her excitedly. "Poor little handsome man," she cradles his body to her chest. "*Mi nene lindo*, my handsome boy." He folds his little arms around his belly and rests his head on her shoulder.

Cutest damn thing I have ever seen, to watch the love between the two of them growing.

We make it to the lake and start building castles out of dirt and twigs, out by the water, that he just steps or sits on. The three of us throw rocks into the water and hunt for birds. Another thing this little man needs to be taught. He's a horrible hunter. But it makes my heart smile.

After we eat our peanut butter and jelly sandwiches and chips, Eli and I lie down on a blanket. Both of us are exhausted from the day so far. He snuggles into my chest and curls into my body underneath the tree, in the shade.

Kat

It is not surprising to find Tank snoring within minutes of lying down, with Eli right behind him. My ovaries explode into dust at the sight of them.

Setting my sandwich down, I take the moment gifted to me, and snap a few pictures of them with my phone. I'm not able to resist, and I lie on the opposite side of Tank to watch Eli sleep. Memorizing this flash in time. It may be all that we have. This perfect moment as a little family.

The future is still unknown. None of us knows what will happen. It will be a fight to keep *this* and keep *us* all together. We can do anything as long as all of us make it out alive.

My fingers run through Eli's hair, pushing it away from his perfect face. I love his chubby cheeks and little nose. I will do anything to keep him safe.

Tank called me *momma* all day long. The sweetest thing he has ever done for me. He is teaching my son who I am. Every time he repeats it to Eli, it cements a little more for him that I am his mom. A gift I can never repay, but I will try.

I'm not sure how long I lie there before Tank wakes up. He swallows and coughs a little. I'm sure it was dry from all the snoring.

"Hey, Kat, everything okay?" he asks with a raspy voice.

"Perfect day," I respond and sit up to face him. "I would be lying if I told you that I wasn't scared, Tank, for the future and what would happen."

"Me, too, Kit Kat, but let me worry about you two. I will be here for you both."

"I'm sorry, Tank, for the things that have happened since I walked into your life. The things that I have done to *you* and *us*," I confess my fear that he won't understand what I did. "I'm not good at telling you everything. The life I lived before was not that way. I was trying to do what was right for Eli, and I ended up hurting us in the process."

I tell him about how I thought I could kill Matias by myself and save us all. About the plans I had to come back to him and be able to start fresh again.

"I was a fool to believe that it would be that easy. I took advantage of your easy-going nature and didn't see the repercussions of my actions. I just assumed you would be okay because it is *you*. Strong, funny and loving." My hand runs over his head and beard. "Will you forgive me? We won't play games, there will be real forgiveness there?"

Laying my heart out there for him hurts because he could just as easily trick me or say no.

"Kat," he pauses. "In case you didn't know, I have been obsessed with you since our first night. I *love* you and Eli. I chased you for a long time, way before I knew who you were. I knew you were crazy as hell when you came back. I'd chase you again for as long as I needed to."

"Love you."

I place my fingers over his lips, not wanting the words back in this moment. I just want Tank to know my feelings, that these words were for him. He kisses my fingers and smiles under their pressure. I move my hand and kiss his full lips, unable to stop myself.

His hand gently holds my head and our faces are inches apart. "Kat, no more secrets between us. Promise me that you will include me in your decisions and choices. We are a team. Let me hear you say it." Of course he goads me into humility.

"I promise to give you everything, my heart and all my secrets." Leaning in, I kiss his nose.

"Good." He smirks like a king and his laughter wakes Eli up.

"Time for a piss." He takes Eli's hand and walks over to a tree where he helps him out of his diaper, tossing it back at me. "No more of these, K-Love, he's a toddler, not a damn baby. What else did those missionaries do to him that I am going to have to fix?" he hollers at me.

Eli just watches, stunned, not sure what they are doing together when Tank stands and pulls his jeans down, explaining everything in detail as he goes. "Point your dick at the tree and not me. You piss on another man, you're gonna end up in a fight. Now, hold your dick like this, take aim and let it happen."

Tank starts pissing on the tree, and, sure enough, Eli copies that too and they pee together, marking the tree. Tank looks over his shoulder and smiles like a proud father. "He's a natural, babe. And not a bad size for a little guy." He pulls his pants back up, then helps Eli with his.

It dawns on me that I have another Tank on my hands, and, God, I don't know that I am ready for that, or the club.

The boys decide that it's hot enough for a swim and strip their clothes off, except Tank leaves his boxers on. He jumps in and swims with Eli for a few minutes, splashing in the water.

The mountain lake water is freezing and it doesn't take long before they are cold enough and come out of it. I dry Eli off with the blanket we brought, then dress him. This time, on our way back, I take the backpack and Eli rides on Tank's shoulders.

I hope that this is where we end up, after the battle of our lives.

Fighting for forever.

CHAPTER 10

Tank

The crisp mountain air lingers with the dense moisture surrounding me in the backyard. The morning dawn shines through the forest and cascades a beautiful picture around me.

Sipping on my coffee, my mind trails off over the past few weeks and the events that led us to today. We've settled in up here, at the cabin, for about a week now, after Kat and I reunited. She has taken the time to spend with her son. A little more peace has settled in and calmed her down, something that Kat never had before.

She and I have talked the events over, and I understand better now how we got to where we are to today. I've made my peace with her past decisions because I knew what I was getting myself into with her. I knew she was a wild card. And I would have done the same to protect Eli, a hundred times over.

It's a complicated mess we have entangled ourselves in. It is moving forward, and that's what I am the most concerned about. Can I forgive my brothers for them not telling me about her plans and keeping that from me when they knew my intention was to brand her as my own?

My gut feels unsettled and my nerves are on edge with the dramatic changes in my world. The biggest of all is killing her husband. He will always be in the background of not only the MC but our lives if he's not killed. That brings me to Kat. Will she back off and let me take care of her and Eli? Sure, we made up, but will she let me protect her? These things need to be settled and, once again, I hate that, in this moment, I can't lean on my brothers for support.

One thing is clear though. I can't keep Kat and Eli here and do what I need to do. I have to take them back to the clubhouse to protect them. If they are found up here, alone and unguarded, then I could lose them both. At least, at the club, there's an entire army ready to protect them, and not just myself.

Walking into the wolves' den is going to be an epic showdown because we have a score to settle. Jane and Kat may not agree, but they are going to have to get on board with it.

Walking in, Eli comes running to me on wobbly baby legs. He makes me laugh and has lightened up my world so much.

"Tank!" he belts. I pick him up, tossing him high into the air. His soft black hair floats behind him. His squeals are a sound that is pure joy. He lands in my arms and makes himself comfortable.

"C'mon, little dude, we have some ladies to piss off." He lays his head on my shoulder and wraps a tiny little arm around it, holding onto my shirt. He makes me feel like a hero. I snicker because it's going to get ugly here in a few seconds.

"Excuse me," I stand in the living room, addressing Kat, Jane and Danny. "Us men of the house have an announcement to make."

Right on cue, my mini me pops his head up in support. "We have to pack our stuff up and head out to the clubhouse."

Jane's mouth opens and she's about to protest, but I hold my hand up. "Jane, I can't protect you guys here and do what I need to do. You and Danny should come with us. I can't make you, though, it is your choice, *but* my lil' man and woman are going, period."

Kat's eyes narrow at my choice of words, but she knows them to be true. This isn't a secure location to do what we need to.

Danny fights a smile because, if I have noticed anything, Jane doesn't get ordered around. She's a great woman, just too prissy for me to take.

"Tank, thank you, but I think that, for the sake of everyone involved, it is time that Jane and I moved on." Danny stands and shakes my hand.

"You won't need help?"

"No, I have several contacts in California to get us to where we need to go to be safe. We are heading to Europe for a two-year mission. You won't need to worry about us." He helps Jane up and leads her to their room.

An hour later, we load ourselves into my truck and the Hoffmans into their van. Cuervo drove it up here and helped us load and lock up the cabin.

Kat and Jane spend a long time talking and saying their goodbyes. Danny plays with Eli and tells him he will be back to check on him later. A very un-churchlike, sour looking Jane says her goodbyes to me as well. I still have no clue what I ever did to this woman to earn her dislike. Not that I really care, because the feeling is mutual, and Europe isn't far enough away.

After a long hug from Jane to Eli, we separate. For good, I hope, because, let's face it, that kind of woman was no good for my son.

I don't even say a word on the drive to our destination because, when I arrive, we are going to have a Church meeting like we never have before. Shit is about to go down.

We pull up to the clubhouse and, for the first time in my life as part of the club, I feel an uncertainty of being here. The anger and resentment run through my veins.

"Kat," I pull her to me and kiss her head, "After we get situated, it may get ugly. Keep Eli in the room, love." She knows exactly what might go down, and, what I love the most is that her face gets an edge to it at hearing my words. If I asked her to, she would face them with me, us against them. She's that crazy for me.

The clubhouse quiets, a deadly silence hovering over the room as the three of us walk in. Some stare stunned because Kat is alive, while others, I'm sure, thought that I was dead as well. *And* a lot of it has to do with the kid that clings to her. They're wondering who he is and how we ended up with a toddler.

Before I leave, I help situate Kat and Eli in my old room, then kiss Kat on my way out in search of my brothers. Blade, Spider and Axl are waiting for me already in the bar area. We are in a standoff and stare at each other.

I took the week and then decided that we either find a way to fight through and work out our differences or, at the end of this, we part our ways. But there is only one way to find out.

Blade, the Prez, points to the room we hold Church in to talk. Four best friends walk in that have always had each other's backs. I don't know that we will come out this way afterward. No one else is invited to our meeting. It's not a typical meeting to discuss business, this will be personal.

The door is locked behind Axl and he goes to stand next to the other three. Spider looks unaffected, like he saw this coming, and, to a degree, I guess he did. Blade assesses me for a second before breaking the ice.

"Brother, I'm just happy that the three of you are okay."

"Physically, we are just fine," I bite out because the memories and ache are still fresh from what happened.

He nods at me, "Why exactly are you pissed at us?"

Ignoring his question, I focus on what I came here for. My hands clench and I relax them.

"I need to keep them here with me until we have this shit settled. We have the same problem, and we can take out the Cartel together."

"Bro, what is going on?" Axl looks puzzled, probably because he hasn't heard the whole story yet. "Why wouldn't you be here with us to work on this together?"

I thought I could do this calmly but I guess my anger is still there. "Because the whole time, these two," I point at Blade and Spider, "Have been calling the shots without the rest of us knowing what they were planning."

Blade's eyes squint at my words. "You *know* that you are not privy to all club business. *None of you are.* You knew that Kat came in to work with us."

"That was before I claimed her, and you didn't even think to tell me," I hit a fist to my chest, "What she was planning on doing. Blade, would you have allowed Vegas to die and kill Johnny on her own for what he had done to her?" My voice rises higher as frustration and anger seep from every word.

"No," he answers, knowing the truth. "Kat has been and always will be different from Vegas. Kat had always held the cards and bargained with us for information or work since she came here. Vegas was hurt *because* of us. Don't you dare talk about her, the circumstances are very different."

I edge closer to him, "I would have fucking told you had I been in your shoes. Because I would have known that losing her would have broken you."

"And the club, Tank?" Blade doesn't let go. "What would happen to Dana or Jenn if Matias got to them next in his attempts to bring us all down? I can't control Kat, that's between you two. You willingly walked into it, taking things on with her, when you knew the score."

"I thought she had *died*!" I roar, "I thought my life was over."

"Tank," Spider calls, "It was me who agreed to help her, not Blade. He's covering for me. Doesn't change what happened, but it wasn't supposed to be that you thought she'd died."

Anger swarms my head and I swing at the wall, punching a hole through the plaster.

"You were supposed to come back to the clubhouse, but, instead, you took off. We didn't—"

Cutting Blade off, I demand an answer from Spider. "What the fuck did you give her?" I roar and charge at him. My fists fly for his face and I land a few before we are on the ground, wrestling on the floor. He can't handle my weight and I sit atop of him with my hands wrapped around his throat and squeeze. Blade and Axl come rushing forward and tackle me, dog piling on top of me to hold me back.

"Calm the hell down, Tank," Blade tries to reason with me. "We had to throw Matias off, get him into thinking that Kat had died, brother. We would've never let him take her. That was the plan."

"What the ever-loving-fuck have you two done? And don't fuck with me right now, it's not the time. I'm about to start killing motherfuckers." My vision starts blurring, and the room starts spinning. "Assholes," is all I manage. And I black out.

Eventually, I come to and Blade is sitting next to me on the floor, with a knife in his hand. "I will cut your ass if you swing at one more person. You hit me, and I will stab your fist." Blade's eyes give a warning that rings true. He tosses me a bottle of water and I sit up with my back to the wall, chugging about half of it.

"What the hell is going on?" My head swims, unsure of what the hell just happened.

Ready or not, Blade picks up where he left off. "We wanted Matias to come and take Kat. She said he would beat her and torture her within minutes of taking her. Our plan was to wait for him, and, when he did that, it'd be there, where we could control it. Fake her death so he would believe he killed her. So that the *Cartel* believed that she was dead."

"You have got to be kidding me! How did you do this?" Kat did tell me what she had done, but I need to hear it from them, too.

"Right before she was to be taken, she swallowed a paralytic and a sleeping pill. Basically, all her muscles, including her lungs, were so relaxed that, unless you looked closely, it would appear that she was dead. If they did happen to figure it out, Matias most likely wouldn't hurt her while she was under. It was also meant to give us time to get to her."

I grab my head and hold on tight while I try to grasp what I've been told. "My woman faked her death. You realize that she was planning on waking up and killing him herself? She didn't think you would protect her. And, guess what? It was me who stopped them from taking her."

"She's like Juliet, man. I thought she'd died, too," Axl takes a seat next to me on the floor. "It worked, though, brother. The scene you made... You know that Matias was watching. He knows she died but you also put a target on your back specifically."

"Good," I grind out, "Let him come for me next. We have a score to settle."

"Technically, she's not married anymore," Axl helpfully points out.

I growl at Axl and Blade points the knife at me, "Don't."

I take a deep breath before I knock Axl the fuck out. "Have you heard from him?"

"No, he's the best at hiding. That's why we had Kat as a decoy. I think he knows about the kid now."

I nod my head, "He knows. Kat saw his men at the house she was hiding their kid in. It's why I am here. I can't protect them alone." I push myself off the floor and they follow me up.

Blade lets out a long breath. "Tank, I knew you cared for her even though she wasn't branded yet. However, you both knew she was a job until this mess was settled. The club is my number one priority."

"Sometimes we mess shit up, brother," Axl tries to reason with me. "When I went crazy, I fucked it all up. Dana and you all forgave me for my shit. Life is never easy. It's not black and white."

I don't say anything because I don't feel that Axl was responsible. I just don't know if I can forgive Spider and Blade yet. That is a real problem with them being the Prez and Sergeant-at-Arms of the club.

"We didn't do shit right by you as our friend, but we also didn't do it just to be assholes to you behind your back. Not to be a dick, but you and Kat had your own part," Spider comments with no remorse.

"Tank, you can't have your personal shit wrapped up in the club. That shit isn't fair to anyone. You both need to talk, too. It's not our job to have Church and discuss what you and your Ol' Lady have discussed or not. Had you not run off, we could have told you that she was okay, and you would've saved yourself a lot of fucking trouble."

"You are a dick."

77

"Yeah, I am. But you knew from the beginning that I wasn't a fan of all this shit mixing together, working together and your relationship. Don't put us in the middle of your personal shit."

"Fuck this shit! You know what? I was there for all these girls, no matter what. Each one of you fucks, too." My finger points at each one of their faces. "We'll finish this war that's been brewing and see where shit is at afterward."

I storm out of the room, not ready to face anyone, and end up in the garage where I would usually be if not at the tattoo shop. Heading to the small fridge, I pull out a beer and chug half of it before looking around only to find Solo watching me.

"Bro, you're back." He wipes his hand on a rag and walks my way.

I just grunt in response because I don't know that I am back all the way or not. "Fuck, brother, I don't know. Everything has been fucked up around here."

"What do you mean?" He grabs a beer and sits on a stool, waiting for me to continue talking. I love this little fucker like he's my little brother.

"C'mon, let's do some of that team building bullshit," he chuckles and takes another swig.

"Solo, I had the heart of a fucking Olympian. Nothing, and I mean not a damn thing, could tear me down. This last year, I focused on the club, and I put me and Kat on the back burner until we could deal with it. It feels fucking cold when you know that your brothers didn't give you a heads up."

Solo watches me intently but doesn't say a word for a few moments. "Tough situation you put yourself in. Can't blame you for how you feel." He takes a drink. "What are you going to do?"

"I'm going to kill Matias and keep Kat and her kid as my own."

Solo chokes on his beer, "Kat has a kid with the Cartel?"

"Yep, but he's mine now. She has a kid with *me*, and we are taking the Cartel down. Hey, I need to talk to Tami. She around today?" The smart kid leaves that alone and takes the hint that I would rather talk about something else, needing to let the anger go for now.

"Yes, she should be home with Cash. You want to ride over there?"

"I do. What about Pawn, have you heard from him?"

With a pained expression, Solo explains, "We *have* heard from him. Tami writes him letters that he gets. But he refuses to see Cash or Tami. It bothers her a lot that he won't see them. He sends me letters addressed to me only and I give them to Tami to read. But they don't really say anything."

"You're not buying into his bullshit, are you?" I ask a little worried.

"No, man, you can't have your life rip apart like that and be okay."

I couldn't have said it better but the next thing that Solo does say means something more to me than he realizes.

"Life is not fair, and forgiveness is needed to survive."

I know he's talking about the three of them. But it rings true for me, too. Nothing that's happened with any of us has been fair, but will forgiveness help me to survive this? If I can't move past my feelings, it could end up getting one of us hurt.

CHAPTER 11

Kat

"I saw Big T yesterday," Tami casually mentions while holding Cash in her arms.

I can't hold back, I really missed seeing this little guy. "Give me Baby T."

Don't ask me why but Tank started calling him that. That man claims everything as his. It's just him, his love knows no bounds. That's why it confuses me that he hasn't been able to forgive his brothers for something that *I* started.

She passes the blonde-haired baby over. He is dressed in a tiny little onesie that has the Battle Born club logo on it. "These are the cutest things that Blade has ever made, other than the twins, Easton and Cortez."

"Seriously, I have to agree." Vegas comes into the common room holding one of the boys, and sits in a chair where Blade sets Cortez down in his car seat next to her. "Thank God Emilia is coming. These boys are draining me."

Vegas wanted to have a club dinner and ordered the guys to barbeque meat. She insisted that Eli met his family, and she wouldn't take no for an answer.

"I think Emilia will be overwhelmed with all these kids to look after but happy."

Dana and Axl come in next with baby Maddison in her pretty little summer dress.

Spider walks into the room with Cowboy and groans, "I remember when we had beer and strippers here. Clothes were also optional."

They both move past, carrying beer and meat to the grill outside where the guys have started on setting up tents so that the rest of us could sit outside with them.

"Thank you," I say to Vegas.

Her eyes sparkle, "For what? You're family." She knows what I mean, this is as much for Tank as it is for me.

"Hey, you never did tell us what it was like working with Spider for a few days."

This time I groan. "He's such a moody asshole. I couldn't wait to get Tank back. While he's obnoxious, he's sweet and fun. Spider is like a moody bossy brother that argues about everything."

Spider hears the end of what I just said when he walks back in. "You only had to argue because you knew I was right, there was no argument. Happy to give you back to Tank to watch over your psychotic ass. I like my woman easy."

"Not true, Jazz isn't easy," I smart back.

He snarls and heads to the kitchen after flipping me off. Axl snickers, "You had to say her name, didn't you?"

"I did. That man needs a little humility and I'll be the first to deliver if needed. Is she coming?" I ask the girls, hoping that she is.

Dana holds her finger to her lips, "Damn it, I did miss something. Vegas, we fucked up."

"Totally, fucked our entertainment up."

It's so nice to be back. It feels right to be here. If only I could get Tank to see it, too.

The girls and I make a salad, then other side dishes, and I introduce them to my baby. They love Eli and everyone has been enjoying talking with him. Tank came back shortly after running out, with wrapped birthday gifts, toy trucks and guns. He had Eli unwrap them all which made the girls swoon in approval and Tank smile like the king that he thought he was.

As we speak, Tank is sitting with Eli in the dirt, explaining the differences in the cars and motors to a two-year-old. God love that man.

Tank

Damn her! Vegas and her little crew of crazy ass chicks. There is nothing I like more than a party. As soon as I heard that we were having one, I thought that I'd give Eli something from me. I hated that he had been away from us for so long. If I pressed Kat about everything, we could have had him here a lot sooner.

It doesn't escape me that these sneaky bitches are up to something. They are showing me what life would be like as a family and using Eli to seal the deal. I feel used. Vegas, Jenn and Dana wave from across the yard. I point two fingers to my eyes and then point to each one of them. I mouth, "I'm watching you."

"Who are you threatening, *mijo*?" Vegas' grandmother walks into the backyard, followed by Fuego and his wife, Cindy.

"Nobody," I play coy and pick the little woman up. "I missed you, *abuela*," I tell her as I keep her in a tight hug. "Come over and meet my son."

The yard falls silent, and, do I give a fuck? No, not at all. He *is* my son because I am going to marry Kat.

Abuela gets lost in hugging all the girls and gushing over all the kids. "I'm stealing her from you," I inform Fuego, and Ghost, too, who joined the BBQ while I wasn't looking.

"You couldn't handle her," Fuego laughs. "She's all sweet and loving looking, but, trust me, that woman came up here to meddle."

"Meddle in what?"

"Oh, you'll see." Fuego, the cryptic asshole, leaves to go see his grandkids.

Kat walks into the yard when she sees *abuela*, and her steps falter.

"Katherine?" *abuela* calls to her, "My little *niña*, is that you? *Mi hijita, eres tu?*"

"*Sí*," a stunned Kat doesn't move until she and *abuela* are hugging.

Abuela pulls back. "I've missed you so much. Why didn't you come to me for help?"

"I didn't want to put you at risk."

"Hold the phone," Vegas interrupts, "How do you guys know each other?"

Abuela smirks and gets a Corona out of the cooler, pulling a chair up. The entire yard moves in to hear this story.

"Many, many years ago, Katherine's mother, Maria, would see Rosa regularly, when Katherine was very small. All you girls played together and loved each other." *Abuela* stops and hands her beer over to Blade who pops the top for her with a smile on his face. Wow, Blade smiled.

"*Gracias*, you are a handsome man, my Alessia did well." She takes a drink and winks at Vegas.

"Anyway, Katherine's mother was the sister-in-law to Cuervo. You see, that is a bond that's bound by blood. But, more importantly than that is that we are bound by *familia*. Maria loved Rosa like a sister and that bond grew tighter than blood. Maria knew that she was in trouble, and I promised to watch over her daughters like I would my own. I've kept my promise because I love my family, and I loved both Rosa and Maria."

Abuela looks at all of us around the yard, with a knowing look. "Make amends when needed, swallow the pride, and show compassion for *tu familia*." And there it is. That's what Fuego brought his mother for, and also for her to see her granddaughter by choice.

"I never lost contact with Katherine, however. I figured out early on that her twin sister was her father's daughter and no amount of love would bring her to me."

We all must be wearing confused looks on our faces. Kat fills in the gap, "We wrote letters to each other for a long time after my mother passed. *Abuela* kept me together, the only person who could understand and help me. As time went on and life changed, I called her and kept in touch. She was the first person to know when I was pregnant with Eli."

Fuego had known, he *had* to. My head snaps in his direction and the devil grins back at me. "An old wise woman once told me to let the ones you loved find themselves in their trials. Give them enough to support them, but also not too much, just enough to keep them ambitious to earn their choices."

Abuela chuckles and agrees, "You see, there is a flower that can only bloom in darkness."

Nosy sons of bitches, and I know the one who did this. Vegas. She loves her husband, the club, and I can't say that I don't appreciate her a little bit for the effort she put into helping us move past this. She's just like her father and grandmother, all scheming meddlers.

The girls huddle in the corner and *abuela*'s words hit me in the heart. She wants us to get along and set aside our differences, keep our bond tight within the club.

Our family.

CHAPTER 12

Tank

The Church room doors click shut before they are locked. It's been a while since we stood behind these doors as brothers, and the doubt that has crept in lately has no room here. There never was that before now, at least not for me.

I've been the Road Captain since we moved here and formed the Reno chapter. I look around at all the men. Saint and Solo are the two newest members that have joined, that I personally vetted into the club and gave my support to. Now, here I sit, swimming in my own guilt from my thoughts about possibly leaving after this is all over.

It feels as if the tables have turned in a way. I feel that Blade and Spider betrayed me by not telling me what they knew. Ironic that I sit here, as an officer seat holding member, contemplating leaving them all behind. It feels like betrayal to me. Withholding any information is lying, but will it happen?

Well, shit, Karma is an ugly bitch.

"Tank," Blade calls for my attention. I have no clue how long I was lost in my own thoughts. "Can you update everyone on what has happened?"

Sitting up a little straighter, I start talking. "Matias, as far as I know, thinks that his wife is dead. What everyone didn't know, was that Kat had their kid in hiding. I think Matias started piecing it together and came here to get her to take him to Eli. That must have been the abrupt reason he came here and took her himself."

"So, *you* knew about the kid? Since when?" Blade's assessing eyes watch me for a while. And, again, it is not lost on me that he is keeping count of my own faults.

"I knew she had someone who she was protecting. Who that was exactly, I hadn't confirmed yet. I told you all in Church but didn't know who it was. When I went down there, after I thought she had died, to move the family myself, I figured out who the kid was."

Solo speaks up. "He did say that, I remember. He wanted help from Spider to confirm who they were." He doesn't see what is happening underneath it all and the question is clearly written across his face until he figures it out, and even scowls at Blade and Spider.

That's not what I wanted, to pit the guys against each other. I hold my hand up. "A lot of shit has gone down, just a missed detail. Kat said that she followed me down there and saw that Matias' men were in fact in the house right after we left. She and Spider took out the guys that were sent there."

Axl and Blade both turn their heads toward Spider. Blade's eyes are as sharp as daggers. "Spider, they know for certain now that we were there watching and that we killed off their members. Matias knows without a doubt that his kid was there. Shit, we declared war on the Cartel."

Spider shakes his head. "Kat was not going to leave until she had her way. Blood for blood. At the time, we thought her kid was gone and Tank, too. She had nothing in this world to lose but her life. If they had really taken Tank and her kid, I was going to help her. And I would do it again." He stares at me when the words leave his mouth, daring me to say differently. In the end, he will always have my back, even if we disagree on things.

Fuego, Ghost and Cuervo sit on the opposite side of the room, listening and reading the depth of our problems very accurately. Not only have we gone to war with the Cartel, but with each other as well. Fuego runs a hand over his goatee deep, in thought.

"It's been a storm brewing around here for a long time. We, the whole club, have been behind on this situation." Ghost nods and Cuervo remains stoic. "We all own a piece of the blame in this hurricane of problems. We, the elder presidents, have made you the center of our club and the storm, no? It would only be right you all held onto your resentment for your losses."

He shakes his head, "Even the smartest of men can miss things." He looks between Blade and me. "You are all still so young and we have forgotten this, yes? I take my part in giving you my responsibilities to fix, *esto también es mi culpa.* Slowly, the fray of your bond started to unravel with every piece revealed along the way."

Fuego sits back and looks at us all with his hands up. "You do see that this, *todos nosotros*, all of us fighting amongst each other," he points around the room, "Is exactly his intent. Pull you apart brick-by-brick until you crumble under the pressure." He slams his fist on the table. "*Esto no esta bien*, do better, and stop it with the blame." His eyes go to Blade, Axl, Spider and then, lastly, me.

He is right, but how do you just let this shit go and walk away from it?

Blade agrees, "We hear you, Prez. Battle Born until we fucking die." He directs his comments at the three of us, Axl, Spider and me.

"Until we fuckin' die," we all confirm at the same time. I know the truth now. I can never leave.

It would be impossible not to walk this life and have our doubts. But the truth always comes out eventually and it is heard.

"*Hasta la muerte*," Fuego and Ghost repeat with pride.

Battle Born until we fuckin' die.

CHAPTER 13

Tank

"What is this?" I ask as I'm walking into the garage the next afternoon.

"Garage party. Team building," Solo confirms with a wide smile. I step closer and give him a fist bump with a half hug.

"This is banging, dude." My brother is the man, this is exactly what we needed.

Jenn has her speakers set up and she plays a nineties throwback playlist. I can't help the smile that creeps up on my face. They went all out for this. The girls are dressed in little plaid skirts or jeans with crop tops.

My Kit Kat wears overalls and a scrunchy thing in her hair. She looks fucking young with those hoop earrings, and I wish I had her even back then. "Lil' momma, you look hot."

Eli reaches for me and I pick him up from her arms. Even he has a little flannel and Doc Martins on. "Bro, you get to hang with the big dogs tonight dressed like a lil' bad-a-s-s."

Kat swats at my arm, "Don't, Tank, he will figure it out."

"No, he won't. Say, *bye, momma.*" I pick up his hand and wave it at Kat, then take my kid to get a drink. She can't stop me. I crack open a can of orange soda and chug half of it before handing it to him, then crack open a beer for myself.

Solo hesitates, opens and closes his mouth couple of times before he finally spits out his thoughts, "Are you supposed to give a baby soda? I'm not sure this is a good idea."

"What about his baby teeth?" Cowboy questions.

"Doesn't he get new ones?" I answer with a shrug and they both shrug back.

Eli takes the soda and tries to drink it as fast as he can but can't keep up and most of it ends up on his face, myself and his clothes. His eyes flare from the flavor and his little tongue licks up what he can.

"Babe," I yell for Kat across the room, "I'm pretty sure those people you left him with," she rolls her eyes at me, "Never gave him a soda, and I just gave him his first." I laugh because I really wish Jane's uptight ass was here to see this.

She shakes her head at me and turns back to her convo with the girls.

"Dudes," this time I address Solo and the rest of the guys hanging around, "*I* am the only one allowed to give him his firsts, his first beer, bud, bitches, all of it, *mine*," I warn them all.

"Bitches," Eli parrots and laughs.

"What the fuck did he just say?" Cowboy laughs.

"Tank!" Kat screeches and starts heading our way.

"Fuck."

"Fuck." He does it again.

I glare at his face, "You messed up, dude." When Kat is close enough, I say louder, "He said *truck*, K–Love."

"Fuck."

She glares and pulls him out of my arms, but he starts screaming at her. "He was better off with those people than you. What's *wrong* with you?"

"That hurts, Kit Kat, deep inside, I know you don't mean it, though," I yell at her retreating back, then watch her wiping his face clean and smothering it in kisses. I'm totally killing this dad thing.

I spend the night hanging with my boys like we used to. Everyone is happy even though we have a big problem still. I can fight anything, though, as long as I have my family. After our meeting last night, a lot has settled in my mind and I realize that we really were getting too far into our own heads and getting on each other too hard.

Fuego and Cindy have each of the twins, and I've never seen a happier man. At some point, Snake, Vegas' brother, showed up, and all I hear is Cindy annoying the man to death about having his own family. Vegas doesn't help and eggs her mom on. Fuego just ignores the chaos, because it's not really, it's the sounds of a happy family.

Axl even has his mom, Harley, here, and, damn, the woman is still fine. She is a part of our crew, just like Tami, now.

I look to where Tami's standing next to me. She grew up and has a place here, she belongs to me, too. I see Solo wrapping his arms around her waist and kissing Cash's forehead. I get it, some may not understand their life, but I do. Eli is mine by choice because I want him, just like I choose Kat.

"What's next, brother?"

Solo looks up at me from the baby. "We are getting married soon. And, after that, hopefully someday, Tami will have another baby."

"Did you ask?"

Solo blinks, "Yeah, I asked her. She has a ring, doesn't she?"

"No, you didn't ask me, the Prez, Axl or Spider for her hand."

"Are you shitting me right now?"

"No," I glare into his face. "She belongs to us, motherfucker. You need club approval, she's a princess. I might let it happen if you can get the other three to approve."

He stares and doesn't blink, waiting for me to move or say more. "May as well get to it." I wave my hand in a grand gesture into Axl and Blade's direction who are standing by their women.

He inhales, taking me a hundred percent seriously, and walks off with determination. My arm wraps around Tami's shoulders, "He loves you, girl, look at that. He's a little stupid, too, FYI. I was only kidding, but I'm not stopping this from happening." My body shakes with unheard laughter while watching Solo.

Tami chuckles, "That is really mean, Big T."

Blade raises a brow at us from across the room and Axl turns and smiles before looking back at Solo with a straight, mean glare. Poor kid, they are going to make this hard.

"It really is, but don't lie, you love it."

"Yes, I do love it. Thank you, Tank."

"For what?"

"Taking care of me and coming back. I wasn't sure you would," she confesses, a little sadness lingering in her words.

"Hey, I couldn't leave my brothers, and definitely not *you*. You okay, though?"

She does a small lift with the corner of her mouth. "It's kind of weird. It hurts that Pawn won't see us or talk to me. I know that things are complicated, but, Jesus, what was I supposed to do? And now his son is *my* son. And I just worry how things will work out, you know?" She heaves after her long rant, and, this time, I just blink.

I may be in over my head here with that one. Her pleading eyes ask for direction from me. I'm stumped. What the hell do you say to that? I've never done any of this before.

"Hey," Kat's hand lands on Tami's arm, "Give Pawn some time. He went through a lot before he went in. The time apart will help him to piece together what he needs, too. Trust me, leaving Eli behind was the hardest but also the best choice for him at the time."

Tami's resigned face accepts the words but still doesn't want the reality.

"We are your family, Lil' T. Kat and I are here for you, always."

Eli comes running up and pulls on my hand. "Excuse me, ladies, nature calls. Come on, E, let's go find a tree."

"A tree? Do I dare ask?" Tami laughs and the guys listen in.

"Yep, it's time to take a piss. Zip it, lil' dude, before you get your mom on my a-s-s."

Turning around, I wink at the most beautiful woman in the world. The woman I waited for my entire life and looked to the ends of the desert for. My K-Love.

CHAPTER 14

Tank

I howl at the sun as we're riding down the deserted highway on our way to Las Vegas. Solo looks like a fresh little chicken out of the roost. The rest of us older guys, however, feel like we've been hit with a million pounds of concrete after all the shit we did last night.

I'm not going to lie and say that I didn't just snort a fat hog up my nose before we jumped on the bikes. I did. At our age, how else are we going to stay upright unless coke sobered us up?

It brings back memories of the times we did that shit on the regular before we headed out on runs. I howl again, and this one is for Maddox. I silently say, *For you, brother.*

Fuck, times have changed. But, no matter what, I learned that if you stick together through the hard times, you become stronger. Battle Born until we die.

The road and the club will always be my home and life. I will never walk away, and I vow to myself to never let those doubts creep in again. I'm a solid *Motha Fucka*. Assholes will never bring me down.

Everyone in my life held me up and waited for me to come around. Until you've lived on the other side of that fucked up coin, you don't know what to expect until you're hit with it. Never again. My brotherhood is a bond never to be broken or tested again.

With Kat, she is my life as well. After the shit that has run us over, our bond, too, is unbreakable. There is nothing that will make me doubt her, us or our family. She is mine and is a part of my blood. There is no part of me that she hasn't consumed. Together, we are one and destined to live this life together. I don't give a fuck if we ever get married. She belongs to me and my brand on her is enough for me.

Don't get me wrong, I will do my best to put a ring on it. I won't leave any part of her left untouched in any way if I can help it.

Tami, too, I have plans for her as well. As soon as I get off this bike, I am going to have a sit-down with Spider, and he is going to help me. The way I see it, he owes me.

And just like that, the road is a balm to my calm and we're rolling up into Stryker's clubhouse. This is the main clubhouse and it's where the big boss himself lives with his woman, Moxie. They are both waiting for us, along with Titan, his VP, on the front porch.

We start removing any leather we can after the ride down. Las Vegas is like an oven during the middle of the day. Titan, that good looking asshole, looks like he's been getting plenty of sun in the back pool with the two club bitches that hang off at his side in the tiniest bikinis I've ever seen.

Moxie hugs her son, Blade, first and then follows up with a hug for all who rode down with us, Solo, Saint and Cowboy. The Prez and I didn't want too many of us gone for this meet with Styker, so Axl, Spider and Fuego stayed behind to keep watch over the girls and club.

"Hey, Momma Mox, I've missed you." I give her a big hug and pick her up and off the floor. My own mother is a bitch, and since I haven't talked to my parents in a long time, Moxie has become like my own, and she keeps track of me, too. I give her credit for the shit she put up with and the way she kept us in line the best that she could.

"Honey, you look so handsome and happy. You have really grown up over these past few years. Every time I see you, you change just that much more. I hate that my boys are so far away." Moxie glares over to her Ol' Man, Stryker, and rattles on about food waiting for us. He ignores her remark and slaps her ass when she walks past him.

"Titan, Stryker." We hit fists on our way through the door and meet Moxie in the bar area where she has food laid out for us. Audio, Jenn's brother, is standing behind the bar, grabbing some beers for us as soon as he notices that we walked in.

It is nice coming back and seeing the old club where we all grew up and where things started. Our roots have grown, but, still, this place is our foundation.

Saint sits down next to Audio at the table and gives him details about Jenn and how she's doing, while we eat steak sandwiches and fries. I notice that Titan absently comments, "She looked and sang really good up there the last time I saw her. She coming back anytime soon?" He asks that only to fuck with Saint. Interesting, I may have to poke into that one a little further and file it away for later.

Saint smirks at his taunt, "She looks even better when she is under me and sounds even better when she's screaming my name. Something you will never hear or see."

"I bet." Titan takes a bite of his food and chuckles while chewing.

After we all had enough to eat and then showered, we meet with Stryker and his officers for a club meeting. The large room echoes with the high ceilings and the space that's not filled with the rest of the brothers.

Blade gives his old man a rundown of it all and leaves nothing left unsaid which takes a fair amount of time.

"Spider has Kat's computer?"

"Yes, he's been combing through all the information she had gathered and even started looking at some other possible leads to help. Now that we know more and who we are dealing with, we may finally get to the bottom of this shit once and for all."

Stryker's face brightens and he leans in, interested. "What do you plan on doing?"

Blade lights up a smoke and hands one to Stryker. "The same exact shit he was doing to us."

Take him down a piece at a time and shatter what he thought was his reality.

CHAPTER 15

Kat

"Eli!" I yell for him to stop. He hysterically laughs but pulls at the door handle as hard as he can and tries to escape out the back door as quickly as possible. "Oh my God, I need to baby proof this house and lock it down ASAP."

I pick the escape artist up, with one arm around his waist. His arms fly in front of him and he squeals, kicking his feet.

"Okay, for one, you were much cuter on the monitor. Two, no wonder Jane and Danny left all the way to Europe. And three, why are you so much better when Tank is around?"

"That's because he plays with him. He needs a friend," Vegas helpfully points out. "Maybe we can make the new prospects play with him and they can take turns?" She laughs and takes him from me, tossing him high into the air.

I fall back against the couch, feeling exhausted. "Maybe that will help."

Since the guys left, we have been forced into lockdown. We all will be living here until the Cartel is dealt with.

"Let's go buy some toys? And maybe some door handle things that lock the master escaper in. You know he is smart like his momma who's always finding her way out of things."

"I'm going to kill Karma if I can ever track her down," I sigh. "We have a problem, though. Are we going to take all these kids to the store?"

"Are you crazy? Hell no. I'm going to get my mom to help watch them. We can take Maddy, she's the best friggin kid. Just sits there. I need a kid like that."

"She is also a girl, we have boys," this time *I* helpfully point out. "All of our problems are because of boys, you know what I'm sayin'?"

We find Cindy and she is more than happy to watch the kids for us along with the help of a prospect because Eli needs one adult to himself.

I inwardly cringe at Blade and Vegas' future. If this is what it is like with one, I can't imagine two of them. Dana is more than happy to get out of the club, and Axl comes along with a growling Spider.

Fuego says, "There is no way in hell I'm watching a bunch of women in a kids' store. I'll stay here with the men."

Walking into the store, we grab a cart and begin running our errands. Can I just say thank fuck that Dana and Vegas had a list and helped me gather food and other necessities that kids apparently need? By the time we leave, we have three carts full of toys, food and clothes. I haven't had this much fun since, well, I really don't know when.

"Did you really need all this shit?" Spider grimaces. "It's like a damn daycare and not a clubhouse anymore. Can we build an extension to house the women and kids only?"

Pushing the cart a little faster than necessary, I clip the back of his boot and heel. "Sorry," I cover my mouth and bug out my eyes for full sassy effect. Spider's glare zeroes in and he grumbles, walking away with a quicker stride.

Dana snickers and adds on louder than needed, "We could totally move into our own space, right after you build it."

Spider flips us off without looking and opens the back of the SUV. To my surprise, back at the clubhouse, Vegas finds a way to get the guys to help us set up a play zone for Eli in the bar area. Boxes and toys litter the place, fitted with things I never knew existed. After they started, there was no stopping Axl's enthusiasm to make it even better. He was bound to build a fort and he took off to the store alone for more supplies.

At this point, it's more of a men's playhouse in the bar, with Nerf guns hidden under the counter. I don't even want to know what they spent on these toys and the camo tent set-up that's taking up most of the space.

Axl proudly holds up a tiny camouflage t-shirt, like his but has a skull on it. "Get the kid, woman, we are ready."

Dana laughs, "I never realized how neglected my man was with the princess and pink stuff."

"It all ends now. I have camo for my princess, too. Dress her, she needs to be a part of this."

"She's six months old, Axl."

"Get my baby out here," Axl threatens Dana with a jab to her chest with a plastic knife. She swats hard at it and it hits the floor.

"I'll get her," she threatens with a finger to his face, "But only because I want you to do your job and play with her, jackass."

Axl's face turns into more of an *adult* kind of mischief and, before he gets carried away, I drag Dana by her arm down the hall with me. The kids have been holed up back here while we were setting up the bar/playroom. I'm sure they are ready to get a break, and their babysitters, too.

Eli just woke up from his nap and he rubs his face with his little chubby paws. "Hey, *bebé*." I pull him up onto my lap and cuddle him just for a minute before I take him to the bathroom. By the time we get back to the bar area, the guys stand in formation, armed with Nerf guns. Axl sternly calls for Lieutenant Eli to come front and center, and waves him over.

Excitedly, Eli runs for him and Axl squats down and removes his little shirt, replacing it with the one he bought for him. The Battle Born men have gone and, in their place, stands an army. Axl arms Eli with a plastic machine gun and a belt with grenades, guns and knives.

"Our mission is to save the princess from being captured," he instructs, holding Maddy in his arms and leading Eli into their camp.

Before long, the girls and I watch a war commencing, and we feed the hungry soldiers sandwiches, enjoying the show. Cowboy is shot in the arm by none other than Spider, who had decided that black face paint was necessary.

"Abort," he hollers out to his men and darts to the back door to leave. You remember the problem I had earlier? Well, we already installed the child locks. He pulls and tugs and the door won't open. He tries pressing the latch above, finally noticing the problem.

"Son of a bitch, what's the trick? I can't get out!" He panics because losing would mean nothing, but his pride makes him play the game seriously.

Axl catches up with him and sends a round of Nerf bullets into his back. The girls and I cheer for Axl's success in saving Princess Maddy.

I got a chance to be something I never believed would ever happen. A mother.

Best day ever.

CHAPTER 16

Tank

The Las Vegas and Reno chapters teamed up with about ten guys to stake out the Cartel Boss, *El Fantasma*, who runs the Southern hemisphere based out of Dallas, Texas. He operates this side of the underground tunnels, from transporting drugs, women and children and cash to whatever else Matias orders. For now, there is a working treaty between the Cartels across the globe, sanctions that network the flow of business.

I'll hand it to Kat. She had a lot of her homework done and she knew that she needed an army for the next phase. Disrupting the carefully planned flow of the underground business. First order of business is stealing this shipment of drugs that's coming to the States which is worth millions after the mules sell it for the Bosses.

From our spot across the street in the apartment we broke into, we watch with our binoculars the people that enter and leave the facility. Walking in, even as an MC looking to distribute and offer a deal, would be deadly. Unless you have the right contact to score an invitation, walking in would put a bullet in your forehead within seconds.

"We need to get in there or get a device in there to hear and see what is going on," Blade comments as we watch several young women unload a bus, with armed guards walking into a warehouse where *El Fantasma* has the drugs weighed and prepared for delivery.

We retreat and head back to the rundown motel the club is staying at, where the group decides that a club girl is needed. Titan is called in and he is immediately on his way down, with one of the girls. The warehouse is kept under surveillance until they can get here later tonight by plane. While we wait, we send the pictures out to all the Sergeants-at-Arms from each chapter. They send us what they can with details on the men in the pictures.

Hector Santiago, one of the top men, frequents his brother's nightclub where he picks up random drifter girls for the night. Santiago has been questioned many times for the same, girls found dead, but was never convicted. He's dangerous but careless, and exactly who we all agree to target. After a review of the girls found dead, we a have one that will drive him wild, a redhead.

Crystal is loud, confident and has legs to wrap around a man for miles. She struts in the door, with Titan as her escort right behind her. We fit her with bugs and GPS tracking devices.

Blade stands by the door before we leave. "Crystal, you could die if he catches onto why you are there—"

A quiet knock raps on the other side of the door, stopping any conversation. We freeze instantly and draw our handguns, pointing them in the direction Blade stands, next to the door. He carefully steps back against the wall and slowly opens the curtain to peek at who is on the other side.

"Open the door," he orders and holsters his gun. Solo first cracks it open and takes a look before swinging it wide open.

There are moments when I shouldn't be surprised anymore but, for some reason, this one floors me. I really should have anticipated it though.

"Woman, is there something *wrong* with you? *Why* are you here?" My teeth grind and clench in frustration. Kat walks through the door, dressed all in black and ready for action. As soon as the door shuts behind her, I bark, "Where is Eli?"

"He's back in Reno. You guys can't get this done without my help."

She walks in, her eyes running over Crystal and ignoring the red-hot anger she has summoned out of me.

"You the bait?" she guesses, questioning her.

Biting my tongue, I don't say another word for now. The guys can't see the anger swirling inside of me for her leaving our son in Reno. I wanted her there safe and *not* here.

Crystal's eyes harden as she looks Kat up and down. "Yeah, and your point?"

"Honey, these men aren't stupid. Flashy tits and long hair come a dime a dozen for them. You smell like desperation. You want to hook him and his interest? Wear something he'll never forget."

Crystal looks irritated but doesn't argue as Kat continues. "You need expensive clothes, money."

Titan and Cowboy chuckle in the background and Kat's furious eyes zero in on the two. "You have a better idea?"

"Kat, she's meat bait. We just need her to plant a device on him," Titan's antagonizing voice laughs at her.

I step forward because I see it happening before he does, and stop her. I know that Blade will see it but hopefully not the rest. I hold her still and grip her arm tightly before she gets a chance to draw the small handgun from around her back.

"Kat," I kiss her temple, "This is Titan, the VP of the Las Vegas chapter," I murmur, hoping that she gets what I'm saying and that it cools her off. I then turn toward her target. "Titan, she knows her shit. Meet Katherine Castillo, and the next time you taunt my woman, we will have a problem."

Kat picks up where she was interrupted and at least leaves her gun in her pants. "She's not a hooker. You want her to be treated like one, then fine, send her out in that." Crystal huffs but Kat keeps up her tirade. "If he sees her in expensive threads, he'll think she's a kept woman and give her more respect than a throwaway *puta* from the street. He'll see money, and sex. The two things these men crave more than anything. You MC boys don't see that need; all you see is a fuck toy."

She steps out of my hold and into Titan's space. The six-foot guy towers over her like a giant she has no problem scowling at from her shorter height.

"Give her a better chance to get out of there without getting fucked up. The best of the two worlds he loves. If she looks like money and then suddenly goes missing, someone will come looking. He will think twice before hurting her, *entiendes*?"

Titan doesn't relent and holds her gaze in challenge. "Let's move this on then and buy what she needs." Stryker agrees and pushes his VP out the door first. Thank fuck, all I need is more drama to clean up.

We escort Kat and Crystal to some fancy clothing store where she takes Crystal in and they try on a few dresses looking like a million-dollar hooker with how little it covers Crystal's body. Kat finds a more modest black dress for herself, with long black sleeves that cover her tattoos. Those sky-high black heels make my dick spring to life before my brain catches on.

"Where do you think you are going?"

"In. I'm watching her from the back. And watching for associates of his that could show up." She reads accurately what my head is screaming. "Suit up if you are coming too, but I'm going in. You walk in with *that* and you'll stick out and be on their radar."

Kat flags over a salesgirl and, before we leave, I'm suited in an Armani disguise. No wonder these guys are all ego. I feel like a king dressed in money. Kat swipes a black card and pays for us, then tucks the card back away before the three of us climb into the back of a rented town car driven by Blade.

Stryker turns around from the passenger seat and tells me, "You're a banking investor here in Texas on business. She," he points to Kat, "Is your mistress, *not* girlfriend and *not* wife, *nobody*."

At this point, she may as well be with how well she listens. Kat sees the fury in my glare that is steaming beneath the surface.

The group of us remain quiet on the rest of the drive over to the nightclub. Rounding the block to our destination, Stryker turns around and watches Crystal closely, "Are you ready to do this?" She nods her head yes. "You may have to fuck this guy to make this look real," he warns because, not only she may not want to, but it may save her life.

"I can handle a little dick, don't worry about it. I got this. We agreed on ten grand. I'll fuck him for that amount of cash," she confirms and smirks. The money, to her, is enough to start over, or is enough to satisfy the greed.

"Ten grand will be waiting for you at the clubhouse."

Blade goes over the plan once more while we wait in the line of cars with passengers waiting to be dropped off. "We are dropping Kat and Tank off first. Go inside and sweep the ground floor. Once we get confirmation that it's all clear, we'll backtrack and drop Crystal off. We only have about two minutes to draw him to Crystal. If he makes it to the upstairs balcony, we may not have a chance."

Kat and I look at each other, seeing a clear solution. "Crystal must run into him on accident, at the doorway."

Kat agrees and, looking at Crystal, adds, "Be submissive and apologetic. Once your apology is accepted, look up and you'll know how to handle the rest." In other words, *Sell your body as payment* is what she didn't say, but the meaning behind her words is there.

Blade pulls up to the drop-off. I exit the car first and hold my hand out for Kat to help her get out. She places her hand on my arm and I pay the guard a stack of cash to let us walk through without waiting in line.

My hand slides around Kat and rests on her hip, guiding her through the large crowd of people. We stand in the back and look around the room of partiers.

"I'm not happy you're here," I tell her in a low voice.

"I know this. But you need me here to make this happen right. You don't know the man you are at war with *or* this world."

Leaning over to her ear, I say loud enough over the music, "You said you would stay safe. You don't know shit about what we know, Kat."

"Do you see me going after him myself? No. I said I want to help, and I will," she bites back at me, staring straight ahead and focusing on her task.

Fuck, she is so stubborn. "Kat, we could've done this without you, and you should've stayed with Eli."

"Tank, I came this far, on my own. There is no fucking way that I will just sit at home now."

"We'll pick this up after this shit is over." She ignores me completely and I promise her in my head that she will pay attention to me later.

We look around for the next few minutes, but are not able to spot our man. I send a text to Blade to send Crystal in. Minutes pass and the crowd starts thickening from the time we walked in.

Crystal walks in and does as instructed, staying at the end of the bar, facing the door. She orders a drink, and we sit and wait. Our patience finally pays off when he shows up about twenty minutes later. Hector Santiago walks in with another associate of the Cartel.

He spots Crystal instantly with her deep throaty laugh that catches his attention. She excuses herself and walks away from the man at the bar. He chases after her and she ignores his attempts at calling for her. The man reaches for her arm and her drink is flung from her hand and onto Santiago's pants and shoes. Okay, that couldn't have played out any better.

Through the crowd, I see her hand flying back and she smacks his face before shoving the guy back. Santiago steps between the two of them, protecting her from the intruder. The man recognizes him and freezes, then leaves without another word. Santiago turns and faces the bait. She looks down and apologizes, looking distraught. His hand grazes her chin and she barely makes eye contact. Perfect.

He whispers into her ear and Crystal's hand grazes his chest. Santiago catches her hand and kisses the top of it and doesn't let it go. Smooth fucker. He tucks her hand into his arm and leads her back over to the bar to buy her another drink.

The only problem is, the guy he brought with him never leaves their side and continually keeps his eyes on her. Crystal plays up the part and hangs off Hector until he eventually takes her to the back room. Shit.

"Go. I'm keeping my eyes on this one. Cover Crystal."

I've never been so conflicted in my life. The Cartel is in the same building as Kat, but I also have a responsibility to the MC. "Go," she repeats and plants a kiss on my cheek, nudging me toward the door.

My feet move and each step feels like a risk. Once I get to the bathroom, Crystal's moans fill the air inside. Through the small slot in the bathroom stall, I see their profiles and her hand slipping into his back pocket where she plants the bug. Since I'm in here, I take a piss and step outside, waiting for them to walk out.

I scan the crowd and look for Kat. Then, my heart jumps in my chest.

Kat

Tank finally left me on my own. I watch as he walks across the floor and disappears into the bathroom.

I have another reason why I sent him away from me. I need to place a bug on this other guy. Finding my target, I push off the wall with the device on my fingertips. It takes me a little longer than I like with the size of the crowd but I weave through the sea of partiers.

Walking with purpose, I move close up on him as he texts on his phone. With practiced fast hands, I slip the small device into his coat pocket and stroll past him without even disturbing the air around.

Successful drop, however, I see that Tank has eyes on me from across the room by the men's bathroom. I don't pay him any attention. I wanted a war, but I never intended to create one with him.

CHAPTER 17

Kat

The door slams shut behind me and the wall rattles with its force.

"You can be as pissed as you want to be, Tank. Point is, you knew the end game here, and it's never been about you or I."

"The fuck it hasn't, Kat! Tell me, if you die, who will raise him?" His voice raises with every word spoken.

I whip around and face him, "You and the club will. He's home, that's all that counts."

His hands fist in his hair. "Why, Kat? Why can't you just let us take care of this and you protect him?"

"Because *I* am the best person to mentally go against Matias. I can't help if I'm miles away. I'm not going after him, *you* are."

He blinks, stunned by my words. "What does that mean?"

"After we have crippled his business and the Cartel Bosses see his weakness, *you* will kill him for me, Tank. He's waiting for me to come after him. He will never suspect me to send someone in my place."

Before he answers, he pauses to think on my words. "What else?"

"If I can't be the one to drive the knife into his skull, then I want you to do it. Tank, he will draw you in and trap you all, and I can't have that happen. I can't lose you to him. If we are going to fight, then we are going to do it together. It's all in or nothing."

He moves closer to me and his hand runs down my arm, holding my hand. "You're scared of losing me again?"

My hand squeezes his, "Yes. I know you can do it on your own. But what if you need me, and I am not here? I can help us win this war."

"I'm not going to stop you from telling me what you know or helping that way. I can't let you put yourself in harm's way anymore, though, Kat, that's my job. I just can't. Eli can't live this life without you. There is no way *I* can live if you aren't on this earth."

Taking a deep breath, he looks at me with understanding. "You want revenge for the wrongs that he did to you." His eyes squint in pain. "I can't imagine what that sick asshole did to you."

My hands run up his suit lapels. I push the jacket off his shoulders, and it hits the floor. I unbutton his shirt next and slide it away from his body. My fingers twist his nipple bar and he moans, then growls with desire.

"Take this suit off, it's not you. I want you, Tank, for now and after this fight. For the rest of my life." I kiss across his chest, my tongue licking at the bar. "I need you. Do you know how hard it is for me to say that?"

His hands stop my movements from removing his pants. Dropping my hands, he fists the hair at the back of my head. "What do you want from me?" he growls.

"Give me his head. Make him suffer knowing that you have my heart and body. Let me help you. Let me *stay*."

Tank slowly unzips the back of my dress with his other hand. "This is all mine? You'll do what I want and need?"

"Yes," I whisper.

"Show me what is mine, Kat." His hurt and anger are lacing his words, and I regret doing this to him. I see it in his face, the stress, and hear it in his tone with me.

His grip loosens and he deadbolts the door, then sits in the chair. The early morning sun barely lights the room. My hands pull the sleeves off my arms and I roll the dress away from my body. I stand before him, bare. I know what he needs.

"I will trust you, and tell you everything, and work with you."

He needs my submission, and, if it weren't for Tank, I would never relent, but, for him, my heart submits. He felt anger because I left our son without telling him. I can't be his woman if I continually make him feel betrayed.

I kneel before him and sit back on my heels, with my head cast down. "My mistake not to call you first.

I was wrong to surprise you. If you made me look a fool, I would take it as an insult. Those are your men."

He hums and leans forward. "We work *together*, or you pack your shit and go home now." He waits for me to respond, and, when I don't move, he requests, "Remove your bra."

My hands do as he asks, and the backs of his fingers lightly strum over my nipples. "I want these pierced for me soon. Every part of you will belong to me."

"Yes, I love you." My heart beats wildly. If he pushed me away now, I don't know if I could handle the rejection.

"K-Love, I will never walk away from you. Stay by my side and be my partner in all things, baby, that is what I need." The tips of his fingers touch over my cold stone heart that he managed to break through. Something so impossible but, like he said, he's the light to my dark. His light saved me.

"I will never abuse your love or trust. We are forever no matter what tomorrow brings. You are the light in my life. You may think you are dark, but, baby, there is so much good, too." My eyes clench at his words, he sees me even when I couldn't. "I love you, Kat."

My hands run up his thighs, and he picks my hands up and kisses each one. "Leave your garter belt on and kneel on the bed."

He helps me up and I pose, waiting for him. He rummages in a bag behind me. The blade of his knife catches the edge of my panties and cuts the flimsy material away from me.

The tip of the knife runs down and scratches my skin down the outside of my thigh, goosebumps breaking out over my heated flesh.

"Has anyone claimed your ass?"

My body naturally tenses at his question, and I remind myself to relax. "No, that has never happened."

"I want it, but I need your trust to take it."

Letting out a deep exhale, I relent, "I trust you." I choke on the last word. Tank's fingers begin to run through my pussy, and they softly stroke, making me forget his last request for a moment.

"Good, we start tonight. Roll over and lie on your back, knees to your chest. I want to see my diamond."

Rolling onto my back, I give him my body. He hums in approval at the sight of the bar with two diamonds on either end that's pierced through my clit.

He holds up a plastic bag and begins to empty the contents next to me with lube and butt plugs of different sizes. My eyes enlarge at the biggest one. "My dick is bigger, but I will get you there slowly." Tank's face holds dark promises

He kneels before me this time, and the irony isn't lost on me. We are a slave to each other. In the end, he will always kneel for me and worship my body with love. His lips leave love bites down the inside of my thighs, priming my lust for him. Reaching my cunt, he puts his hands on each side, opening me up more and taking a long, slow lick, then places a kiss on his diamond.

Thick fingers glide in and out of my pussy while I squirm underneath him. His mouth makes love to my body, sucking and licking at my clit. My body is craving so much more of him and what I know he can give me. My temperature rises, and I pull my legs back more, opening wider, inviting him to take it further.

Tank's finger glides down and he spreads my lust around my asshole, massaging the area gently. A moan escapes me, "More, Tank, give me you."

Something cold presses against my ass as he pushes and turns what must be a plug, at a slow pace, while he continues his attention to my clit.

After a few pushes of back and forth, the first plug is easily seated. He moves to the next one and I'm so close.

"Fuck me, Tank, make me come for you," I plead because I am right *there*, and it won't take much.

He fucks my ass vigorously with the plug and I come for him hard like I never have before.

"Holy shit."

I thought he would be done, but he doesn't let up and keeps licking at my clit and sucks on my pussy lips. Quickly, I build up again, and it feels like something is missing. "I need more Tank."

He chuckles, and I feel the cold end of a plug before he starts the same process again, except, this time, it is larger and takes more time to work it in. He slows his administrations on my clit, and I huff at him, wanting to come again. My eyes pop open when this plug makes it way inside and at how much different it feels, the pressure that much greater. It instantly lights a fire inside that I have never felt.

"Oh fuck," I moan for him. He pumps the lubed plug in and out, fucking my ass, and my stomach begins to clench. "Oh shit, don't stop," I beg, and he doesn't. I come harder than before.

As I come down from the second orgasm, he covers his cock with a condom and adds more lube. "You're ready for my dick. Roll back over onto your hands and knees."

My legs feel weak, but I present my ass to him and bend over on the bed. Beads of lube fall and coat my ass as his dick runs around the area.

"It's all about fucking my K-Love."

Leaning over me, he tugs at my nipples and then holds his dick at my entrance. "You ready?"

"Yes, Tank, claim my ass as yours."

He lets out a throaty growl as he slowly glides into my ass. At first, it feels awkward until he slowly pumps back and forth. His hands grip my hips, and he gives me soft and slow until I adjust, and what was awkward before turns into a lust only he could create. My body pushes back, and he picks up the pace. My skin breaks out in a sweat and the craving intensifies with each pump.

"Fuck, Kat, this ass is fucking tight. You come, and I won't last. So fucking perfect." His hold tightens and his thrusts become hard and fast.

"Oh shit, Tank, fuck me hard," I demand, and my body gears up for the best orgasm. My pussy clenches and I feel a release of fluid leaving my body from the contractions.

Tank pulls out, ripping the condom off and jacking off until cum paints me. "Fuck," he roars out before diving into my pussy.

He is on a mission and doesn't stop until after my fourth orgasm, and after he comes a second time. The man is a machine and his endurance is nothing I have ever seen. He wraps me up into his body, completely satisfied.

Team building fucking rocks.

CHAPTER 18

Tank

Spider's evil gleam radiates from across the room. Those bugs we planted last night worked, and worked really well. Matias, the Cartel Boss of Mexico, has a drop planned of ten kilos of coke and other drugs coming in. At the drop, he will have ten million waiting on a hard drive encrypted with electronic bank numbers for payment.

Since the digital world exploded, cash is no longer usually handed off in bags like in the good ol' days where you had to pay a cleaner to launder the money. Now, the techies of the world push it around in accounts that are harder for the Feds to detect if done right. If your tech guy is a dumbass, you'll land your ass in the Federal Pen.

The other difficult part with the electronic world is if you've never met. Who really is on the other end of that bank transfer? Could be a Fed, or it could be us. If today goes right, we'll have ten million worth in street product and the hard drive with ten million loaded on it for payment. Twenty million dollars in a day's work. With great power come great consequences.

Next door to mine and Kat's room, Spider set up command central where he sits with his glasses on and he and Kat type codes in. Their fingers fly across the keyboards, making or breaking codes. I don't fucking know, but my girl is fucking genius level smart. I'm her muscle and fucking proud to be her hero.

She changes a screen and looks over at the rest of us. "Contact said that Matias left to meet the Cubans on the Coast. Matias hasn't checked in at home in Mexico City in weeks. I think he is still here in the States. This may be easier than I thought."

"Why is that?"

"If we go to Mexico to kill him, he has more allies to help him. Here, he has less, and don't get me started on the crossing the border." She goes back to typing and ignoring us.

We load guns, knives and smoke bombs, anything you can think of, we got it with us. Stryker and Blade review the property on the Coast and how we are going to confiscate and kill everyone. If they see our faces or any markings, we expose the club for being dirty. An unsanctioned attack and stealing a payload. We could lose everything today. No one would want to deal with us, and it would essentially put a target on all of us. Reapers would crawl up from the depths of the belly of the underworld to take us to hell.

"Bring me the cash and product. Do not stay on the main roads. Fuego and Cuervo called in a favor, and their cousin who is a rancher is going to let us set up shop for the next phase."

Solo asks what we all are thinking. "*What* is the next phase?"

Stryker smirks, "We rip off a few more deals, making him look unreliable. He loses credibility and we plant the stolen drugs on his property and tip off the other Cartel Bosses. Then we transfer the money we stole into an account under his name, making him look like he stole it all. They'll want him dead and hopefully kill him for us. If we do kill him, they won't come looking for us because there will be too many Cartel Bosses looking for payback."

We load up our supplies and place trackers in all of our clothes in case any of us goes missing. Kat stands from her chair and pulls me to her, planting a fat kiss on me. "Go be bad today, baby."

My hands squeeze her ass cheeks hard, nipping at her neck and whispering into her ear, "See you soon, Kit Kat, behave." With a slap to her juicy ass for good luck, I'm pumped and determined to make shit happen.

The ride down to the Coast is muggy from the rain and miserable even at night. Our sweat permeates the back of the van that has no windows to ventilate the space.

Once we arrive, we surround the abandoned docks and set up our positions for our drug heist. Jesus, I thought some of the shit we did before was crazy, but this kind of business is a whole other level.

Two black SUV's pull up with Matias' men ready to take the shipment. We watch the men get out and they open the back, ready to load when the boat docks.

Tricky business, we don't know the number of men on the boat and we essentially have to overtake them all at the same time. Instead, we are going to wait for the shipment to be loaded and tested, then take the money and the drugs on one side.

The men shake hands and the drugs start getting loaded while one of them checks the quality of the shipment. Matias' man signals the driver over. He gets out, carrying a briefcase, and is about to hand it over to the Cuban Cartel. Saint, the ex-military sniper, takes aim and shoots the Cuban in the arm.

After the first shot, chaos unleashes, men scramble for cover and bullets fly. Saint aims to hurt and not kill. The same for us, we need a few to survive. We target the rounds up the middle, pushing both groups back. They help us by killing each other off and the men scatter. Eventually, they jump into the SUV's and the Cubans back into the boat and leave with a handful of men.

Two of our men stay behind, while me, Blade, Stryker and Titan take off after the car with the drugs. We fly up the back-dirt road to catch up to the drug caravan. I pull the mask down over my face as we get closer, and, when we are right behind them, we gun it to separate the two vehicles and swerve, hitting the first SUV we pass. It dives headfirst down a steep ravine and gets stuck. We continue the chase after the other one and pull out the machine guns, firing at the back until the tires deflate, causing the car to swerve and slow down.

We speed ahead in the other lane and, from the passenger seat, I shoot the driver in the head. The SUV rolls to the right and flips itself upside down.

One dirty deed done and several more to go before the end, and, hopefully, a new beginning.

CHAPTER 19

Kat

"Cervantes," my ice-cold voice greets one of Matias' men on the phone. "It is time you paid your debt back to me. I have the missing drugs from the drop with the shipment from the Cubans."

Stryker, Blade and the rest of the men listen in while I blackmail the man to do our dirty deeds.

"I was hoping you were dead, *puta*. Seems the *jefe* is weaker than I thought if you are still crawling around on this earth like a *pinche perra*."

I laugh into the phone. "*Cálmate, cabrón*, keep *tu boca* shut, or *tu jefe* will see all your skeletons you have hidden. *Entiendes?*" He doesn't say another word because he has been skimming cash and drugs from Matias for years. He needed money for his gambling debts. The only useful information my father gave me that has ever helped me, that is before we killed him. I kept digging more dirt on him and kept all the information needed to seal his fate, the horrific death of a traitor.

They call the Cartel men the Cursed Kings, like pirates of the mainland. The money is their treasure, there is never enough, and power becomes their obsession. Their lives are empty, dark and decrepit ships in the night, searching to conquest and conquer. Looking for their lost souls in the money they take.

"*Qué quieres*, what do you want?" A lesser woman might hang up at hearing his barbaric tone. Not me. He's scared, as he should be. He's on the losing side and knows it.

"You will meet my men and accept the load. Stash the drugs away in Matias' warehouse and keep it between us. Or I email Matias your bad habits."

"You better know what you're doing, *cabrona*."

"I know exactly what I am doing. So sweet, your concern." I give him the details of the meet in Mexico and hang up the burner phone.

It is risky and deadly. But we came up with a contingency plan, and, if he betrays us, we will send the details I have, plus implicate him in stealing the drugs and building his own small empire behind his boss' back.

After I'm done, Styker calls in his own favor from a local kingpin who distributes for the Cartel. Stryker saved his life years back and the man owes him a debt. They reach a deal where Stryker offers him more territory to sell in if he runs the drugs into Mexico.

That's how the Prez got his road name, he strikes when least expected and always at the best time. Then, you fall at his feet to do his bidding. A few brothers are sent to guard the man's family. But he knows not to fool himself. If he crosses Stryker, he will come home to find his dead wife and children.

As assurances are made, a bomb is placed in their clubhouse bathrooms, kitchen, garages and bar. It may say household cleaner on the containers, but those bombs will clean up the rest of them if he makes a mess of the deal.

There is no loyalty when it comes to thieves. It is not an *if* but a matter of *when* you will be double crossed. You just need to make sure they are prepared to know the retribution coming their way if they decide to do so. Make it hurt and take it all in the ashes of what is left when it is all done.

War.

Battle Born.

We don't communicate with names but through keywords until the shipment is delivered and the kingpin of Texas is back, and he's paid in part with drugs and Matias' money. Ironically, we are taking Matias down with his own cash and blow. Another funny thing, the money paid could point to him as the thief if we want it to. It's a dirty game to play, and, to win, sacrifices must be made.

We move on to the next shipment, and the next, but we keep vigilant for the snake in the grass. I know he's on to us because, even though we may be miles apart, Matias finds ways to send me messages. He's very clever and I'm waiting for his move because it *is* coming. We all know he will gun for us soon.

I keep the details of the encrypted messages to myself because, how do I explain the song we danced to at our wedding on repeat through the streets of Texas to these men? He wants me distracted, careless so that I give him clues and play into his tricks. I won't buy it. I know what he ultimately wants.

It is not the Battle Born territory anymore, his focus is to kill *me*.

I splash cold water onto my face and clear my head. Keep moving forward. It will all work out. I've been telling myself this for days now, all while keeping my shit together.

That is until I receive an email. My hands freeze on the keyboard and I know without a doubt the attachment will tear my world apart. But how badly? My finger taps on the table and I steel myself before finally pushing play.

The screen blinks from black to the faces of the beaten Hoffmans. The torture and death of Jane and Danny, of days' worth of collecting the different scenes into one very horrific movie. The video was filmed days ago. But I know they had made it to Europe because she called me right before this happened.

My chest heaves in pain. They were to never be hurt in this war.

"Kat, what is it?!" Spider's raised voice snaps me out of my trance and over to him. He pulls the laptop to him and pushes play. I turn my back to it because I can't watch it again, but he unmutes it. The cries and screams that fill the air don't set me off, what does is when Matias says, "Happy Anniversary, *mi amor*. I hope to have my family back together soon."

Panic sets in like a high from a drug overdose. My mind spins and the world gets blurry. I scramble up from the desk and to my bag, ripping out everything I have in it. I'm so lost in my head, I don't even realize that I ripped off what I was wearing and dressed back into all black clothes, then started arming myself with guns and cash.

"Kat," Tank yells for my attention. "It is a video and it's bad what happened to them. But calm down! I need you *here*. We'll get him!"

"You don't understand," I hysterically cry. "He has been playing our song over and over to make sure I would hear it. He waited until our anniversary to strike. He is ready, and he is coming *today*. It's his idea of a gift."

"What the fuck are you talking about, Kat?" Blade steps over, along with Stryker, but there isn't enough time for me to stop and explain more.

"He is going after Eli. He may kill him as a gift to me. Jane had to tell Matias where Eli was. Did you not hear her under the screams from Danny? She said, *'I'm sorry, Eli, he's coming.'* He fucking hunted her down and tortured her because of *me*!"

This pain is the torture only one Cursed King could inflict on me. Matias Castillo.

My husband.

CHAPTER 20

Matias

"*Está aquí*, is he here?"

I know my Katherine isn't in Nevada. My sources tell me that she is in Texas. Smart *pinche hija de puta*, stupid cunt, is fucking with my business. I'm taking my son, and, depending on how she responds to her surprise I had done just for her today, he lives or dies. Today.

I never wanted kids of my own. I got her pregnant only to control her. But then, she left me because of the little *bastardo*. Maybe I will keep him alive as long as she does what I want and comes along quietly. I could turn him into her worst fear and make him more ruthless than even I have ever been. There's a thought.

"*Sí, señor*, he is in the care of the MC." This displeases me, that she would leave my pure blood with such garbage. She will pay greatly for everything she has done, and death is too good for her.

"Kill who you have to, and bring me *el niño*."

Solo

"Tami, can you grab me a beer while you are in there?" I grab her hand as she walks past and place a kiss over her engagement ring.

She bends over and places a kiss on my lips. "Only because I love you."

"Love you, too."

Her hand runs across my chest and shoulder when she leaves. Cash is inside the clubhouse, napping, and we brought Eli outside to play in the sun. He runs over to the swing sets we bought and put together recently. Axl and I went overboard and bought even more shit then necessary, but we figured that all these kids would use it at some point.

The sound of footsteps echoes off into the distance. I'm not sure what alerts me into action, but I jump to my feet and draw my gun, pointing it in that direction. My heart pounds and my eyes dart around. Eli laughs and goes down the slide. Next, the sliding glass door opens, and Tami is about to come out.

"No!" I yell at her. "Go back inside." She pulls back but stops. Realizing that Eli is still out here with me, she darts for him. I chase after her and that is when the man dressed in black emerges and aims for us.

She grabs Eli on the run and his little body flies from the abrupt movement. I shoot to give Tami cover as she rushes back into the house, and the guy goes down with a bullet to the chest. But more come at me and I am outnumbered even with Axl's help who I heard running from around the house. I hide behind a picnic table that I pushed over. Axl stands behind the garage wall and pops off a shot, killing one more.

"Lock the house down!" Axl growls at Hitch, an older member.

I see two men round the back side of the garage, looking to take Axl out. I can't get a good shot from where I am crouched down, so I stand and send two bullets into their chests.

"Get the fuck down," Axl screams and points his gun in my general direction.

Searing pain like fire lights up my chest and I fall, first to my knees. I look up to the glass door and the beautiful angel who has tears in her eyes, trying to fight Cuervo off her to get to me. But he holds her back. Why? My hand reaches for her. I want to get up and go to her. My body won't work, though, and my arm drops like dead weight. What is happening? My vision blurs and I can't breathe when I start choking on my own blood.

My world goes dark.

Tank

"Kat, you can't go running right into his trap. How many fucking times are you going to die, woman?" She panics more and paces the room. "We can't head back to Reno. He is drawing you out to distract us and find you. Fuego can take Eli and protect him. Trust the club, Kat. We are on the same fucking team. Now snap the fuck out of it."

Kat is gone and the Black Widow stares deep into my eyes. "If you try and stop me—"

"You'll what? Put a bullet in my head? Fucking do it already, Kat."

She glares and breathes fire with each intake. "I won't lose my son."

"Then snap the fuck out of it! I promised you once that I would protect you even from yourself, and I meant it. Go against me. I dare you." One step forward and then another until I have her pinned against the wall. "Submit," I demand.

It will take a lot to reach her, and I am not sure, with all the shit that has been programmed into her head, that it can ever be fixed. One thing I do know, though. Kat needs to dominate, and she needs to feel in control.

Her husband would beat the submission into her. I won't ever do that, but I have no problem tying her up with love.

When her eyes close, she silently relents. I bend forward and relax her with a kiss on her forehead. "Come on, K-Love, we have work to do. Calls to make and a small dick to find. Get back on that computer and track him down like only the Black Widow can."

What I don't tell her right away is about the call we received from Axl. The Cartel ambushed the house. Eli is safe. But the rest might destroy her, so I hold that piece for now.

CHAPTER 21

Tami

Facing the same window that I watched Solo die from haunts my soul. My hand rests on the cold glass and I stare out into the back yard. The cold is welcome and feels normal as it's seeping into my flesh. The world has no color. Night and day have no meaning to me anymore. I want to hate Kat for his death. If Eli wasn't here, Solo would still be alive.

We weren't even able to have a funeral for him because of the fear that we all could be gunned down for standing out in the open, and, worse, as a group. I hated them all for that.

My heart, whether I want it to or not, is pulled back to that one night a month ago.

My body shakes with fear as I watch a man creep up behind Solo. "No. No. No." I grip the handle of the door, about to rip it open, to yell at him to get down.

But Cuervo stops me. "You want him to aim that pistola at your head?" His strong arms wrap around me and hold me back from saving Solo.

"Let me go! They are going to kill him," I plead as I watch my worst nightmare unfold before my eyes.

In that next second, Solo falls to his knees after a shot is fired, and his hand reaches for me. I swear he said, 'I love you', right before he hit the dirt. The shot sounded like thunder that shattered the course of my life. My heart just died with him. Harley comes to my side and gently pulls me away from the sight of him lying in his own blood. I can't even say why I go with her.

My body shakes from the agony and shock, and she rocks me back and forth where we sit. I crumble into nothing. From the first time I met him, he took my sorrow and buried it and gave me wings to fly. And now he's in heaven.

I don't remember anything that is said, just Harley's soft touch and presence that I crave. I can't take it. She is my beacon and I follow her. Needing someone to pick up the pieces where they fell.

The agony breaks the dream and my head jerks, but before I can stop it, my mind drifts away from me again. A prisoner of my own thoughts, and the flashbacks stay on repeat...

Axl and Fuego stand by the side of where they buried the man I had promised my life to.

"After this is all said and done, we will get him a headstone, I promise." Axl's arm gives me a half hug while I stand in the graveyard. I nod at him in understanding.

Words and feelings have left me, like him. *I stare at the grave that's marked with an almost undetectable, small, white cross. That is it. The only thing to show for his life when he had been so much more. A white cross.*

In darkness, I look up at the stars that shine so bright, where I am sure that he is now. I've cried so much that I am surprised more tears fall like a river down my cheeks. The unmarked grave feels disrespectful toward him. That this cruelty exists disgusts me, because he deserved everything.

We *deserved everything.*

Axl and Fuego stand back and I sit in the grass next to the fresh dirt pile in the graveyard.

"Hey," I whisper to a ghost, "I don't know what to say. We were robbed of our promises, and I can't live. I feel dead inside without you. I have Cash, and I guess he is the only thing keeping me from completely falling into oblivion."

I rip the grass that is poking at my fingers and toss it aside. "You blew me away, Solo, with your love. You taught me what love was. You gave me the first ride on your bike. You were so many of my firsts. I was so many of your firsts, too."

My fingers twist the ring on my finger around. "I wish I could lie down beside you and wake up to your face in the morning, just one more time. Sometimes I dream of our wedding and I wake up crying for you, alone."

I talk to him for hours and pray that he hears every word. I hold on to the ring that I bought for him, that is now on a chain around my neck. Some moments I just cry and others I scream at how pissed off I am at everyone. There isn't a person whose name I don't curse and blame by the time I am done.

"I promised you always and forever, Solo." *My voice croaks but I have enough left in me to rasp,* "Your soul is a part of mine, and, for now, that is all I have. I'll spend my *life wondering what our story could have been." My eyes grow increasingly tired and I close them just for a moment. They feel so heavy and are painfully swollen.*

I wake to my body being lifted and wish I would have died there. To lie with him, to be left beside him. I am taken away from the cold, wet grass and to my family, the Battle Born MC. And the executioners of dreams and happily ever afters.

Solo blew me away on the day we met and he just buried himself away with my heart.

CHAPTER 22

Kat

Tank and I are sitting outside where he just told me the horrible news. Solo has died because of me, too. I want to be angry for him not telling me right away but days later when they buried him, without a funeral, with only a few members at his side to say goodbye.

My head hangs down to my chest. Desperation, regret and fear take me down their deadly path. This is what happens to people at this stage in the game. I killed everything important to Matias to bring him down to his knees, and, literally, he is doing the same to me.

The violence has caused so much grief and evil that it has consumed us all like a virus. The victor gets to live with it all. What a prize and badge of honor to be left with.

"Hey. You did what you had to. This was going to come to what it has at some point. You saved more lives than killed in the long run." Tank holds the tequila bottle out to me, and I take it from him and drink the fire.

"Tami. Will she ever talk to me again?" I ask because I really want to know. I need him to reassure me that I won't lose her.

"No way will she blame you for being a mother who protected her baby. Kat, she *ran* out there and grabbed Eli when bullets were flying. She's not going to blame you."

My head falls to his shoulder and I wrap my arms around his much larger one. The feel of his strength and the heat from his body are a comfort to me. Somehow, he transfers what I crave, forgiveness.

"How are you?"

Tank rests his head on top of mine. "I'm hurting, Kat. I loved that kid. He was my brother. He and Pawn were my little pups and I was teaching them how to run with the big dogs. I feel like I failed him somehow, and Pawn, too. I brought them into the club together."

"Remember the first time they saw Tami? It was like something struck them both like lightning." I blink the tears back.

"Yeah, the three of them had this bond we all could see but they were too scared or too young to see it?" Tank's chest heaves. "We would sit around in the garage and talk, and I would teach them how to be a team. I'm gonna miss him, K-Love."

"Me, too, Tank. I'm going to miss the hell out of him, and I vow to make Tami's life better. She needs love, Tank, the kind that makes the world believe in miracles. I'm going to help her find it."

Tank's arm wraps around my shoulders and he pulls me close to his body. "Kat, this is going to get bloody. I am going to torture Matias like you have never seen in your life. I need you to understand that and not see me as a monster. There is no other way for me. I can't survive this kind of anger without finishing this in the ugliest way possible."

"I'll be there to support you, whatever you need." My hold tightens around his body just as the call we have all been waiting for finally comes through from the Carson State Penitentiary. It was difficult getting him a burner phone on short notice.

Tank

Kat and I slide off the bench outside and walk into Spider's hotel room. That's where I answer the call. I place it on speaker, setting the phone on the table. Stryker, Blade and all the other guys join us around it.

"Pawn," Blade starts speaking and tells him everyone who is in the room. "We have news that you need to hear. Solo died from an ambush from the Cartel. Tami and Cash are okay and are staying at the clubhouse."

The silence in the room is paralyzing. The group hangs their heads and we wait for Pawn to process the news. "How is she doing alone?"

"Not well," Blade gives the full story in detail to him. "She'll get better. We will help her get back on her feet and make sure that Cash is okay."

"I can't help with him. Fuck." Heaviness coats his words. "I- uh- shit, I can't do anything. I can't say goodbye to him. He's been my best friend." He takes a moment and requests, "Make that fucker pay."

"Aye, brother."

Pawn says he has to go, that his time is up, and I can't blame him. I don't want to talk about this any more than he does.

Looking around the room, I demand, "Matias is mine to kill, and he *will* die after I am done torturing him." My gaze stays firmly on Blade and Stryker, the Presidents of the MC. If I have their approval, then it is done.

They both nod with approval at my request, and Stryker grips my shoulder, "We are finishing this to the bitter end. No more tears." He, too, holds each man's gaze. "Remember who you are and what you are. That you pledged to me and what the wolf symbolizes. Strength, leadership, intelligence, protection and, most of all, destruction. We savagely take what we want and make no apologies for it. Life and death are a part of this world. Let the guilt go. Remember who we are, a pack of killers and protectors."

CHAPTER 23

Tank

I can't lie and say that losing Solo hasn't left a dull ache among the brothers. Kat has definitely felt the repercussions of this life as well. She suffered at the hands of cruel men for most of her life. He tried his best to strip her down, but she still fights. Never giving up.

I watch her as she takes the pain in and allows it to consume her. Then, she accepts it, like a warrior.

Kat and I have called Tami as much as we've been able to. Tami never has anything to say. The shock hasn't worn off and she hasn't healed from the loss yet, if she ever will.

It pains me to see these women struggling through this life. In a perfect world, we should have been there to protect them from all this. I would do it for them. Take away all the hurt, like a savior, and bear their struggles as my own. Truth is, none of us can escape life, the good or the bad.

The memory from last night comes back to me, when I held Kat to me while she cried in my arms.

"Be patient, K-Love, I will get us all through this."

She is curled up in a ball and my body wraps around hers while hers is shaking with sobs.

"Pawn was never supposed to go to prison. Solo should have never died while protecting my son. I feel like, had I stayed away, this would have all been so different." She gasps for air, "I want to take it all back."

My hand runs through her hair, "No, you don't. Because you have kept Eli alive. Matias was already coming for us. Some roads, baby, are meant to be travelled. You may not understand them now, but how and when things happen in their own time isn't always clear. Don't question your road or the past. It is what has led you to the woman you are today. Be brave and have faith in yourself and the road. Take every step with confidence, not with regrets."

Her arms wrap around my body and her face is buried into my chest. She places a soft kiss over my heart. "You are the light to my dark."

Kissing her forehead, I tenderly confess, "You are the light to my dark."

Truth is, Kat is fearless, and she has given me more love than I have ever felt in my life. She has seen more pain than I could ever imagine, and, even though she mourns the loss, she stays strong. Even with her hard exterior, there is a tenderness she has kept away from others. I feel it when I am around her. It was only meant to be mine.

We haven't seen Eli for a few months now. Fuego took him, along with his mother to care for Eli, to a safe house that not a person knows where it is. Fuego has a burner phone for us to contact him only in emergencies. The girls have also been separated and placed in different locations, for protection. None of us wanted us to chance anyone's safety.

So far, we have confiscated and placed several shipments back into the warehouse in Mexico. Calls are being made, asking questions, and, for now, distribution has stopped in this area. Bosses are pissed with the lack of product being distributed. No drugs, no money, and they have bills to pay.

The Cartel is starting to self-destruct. The pressure is on for answers, and Matias is on the run now, a hunted man. It is only a matter of time before they find the drugs in his warehouse in Mexico.

"Tank." Blade walks into the room we've been set up in with Spider. "I need you to do some recon." He explains that he wants me to go with him to survey a meeting happening with the Cartel.

Kat and Spider are busy at work, still on the computers, so I step outside with Blade and Stryker.

"Matias is in Texas and looking for Kat," Blade informs us. "Cowboy got confirmation on the street. He knows now that we are behind the drugs and stashing it into his warehouse. Matias also knows that Kat has connections on the dark web. He isn't going to come for her there—"

"Until he is ready to bait her into another ploy," I finish for him. "We can't tell Kat. She'll get boots on the ground and go after him herself."

Stryker nods, "Agreed. Spider and the men know. We are going to go look at where Matias is hiding now. Plant some trackers if we can and set up any surveillance. And then wait for him to get in contact with Kat."

Some wars are meant to be won by sacrificing the queen.

Matias

She whimpers underneath my hands that are wrapped around her throat. I release one hand and smack her across the face with all the force that I can, wishing it would knock her out and she would quit her sniveling.

These stupid white *perras* are the same. One after another, they have not satisfied any thirst I had for sex. Mexican, pure blood *mujeres Mexicanas*. One in particular I crave, and have craved for years, and until I get her back, I will continue to break the spirit of this woman to do my bidding.

In the last week, I've beaten her regularly until I felt satisfied that she gave me every detail about Katherine. Now I know everything and, best of all, where she is. It doesn't surprise me that she accomplished what she had. The woman is smart. I just can't figure out why.

"Don't cry, *pinche guera*, stupid white girl." I slam my dick into her with all the pent-up anger swarming around me that I can't get rid of. Closing my eyes, I picture Kat, how she looked before she left me. Those prized moments of when I thought we connected.

I pound harder, my release drawing in, and Kat's dead body lies beneath me. Her eyes open, mouth hanging open. The bitch's hands lay hazardless by her sides. Moaning, my dick shoots off, finally, and the stupid little *perra* whimpers again, destroying my fantasy and pulling me back into the present.

"*Puta barata*, cheap whore."

Shoving her away from me, I rip the condom off my cock and throw it into the trash. I watch her bleeding on the bed. "Clean this up," I point to the bed and her disgusting body.

After I have showered her filth off me, I get back to my business. My men have confirmed that the shipments that had gone missing were tipped off to be located in my warehouse. Many pissed off Cartel Bosses are now looking for me, the Cursed Kings want their payment, and they also want me dead.

There is only one way out of this. Capture Katherine and get the evidence I need to clear my name. My future is a ticking time bomb and I need her alive. My first step was killing that little puke of a man at their clubhouse.

My target was Eli, but that was a fail. Second best was the man she left to care for him. At least when I pulled the trigger, I felt some relief for all she'd taken from me.

This should be enough of a distraction to lure her into my next plan. Katherine will sacrifice herself to save someone else.

Tank

My heart is pounding in my chest as I watch Jane walking across the room after Matias left, naked and grotesquely beaten, with large black and blue bruises littered across her pale skin. He never killed her, and now we know how he is going to bait my Kit Kat. Shit, I wish I could put a bullet through Jane's head from where I'm sitting because, by the looks of it, after this, she may never survive in this world again.

Unfortunately for Jane, she has become a pawn and has to be sacrificed for the end game, killing Matias. The brothers and I pass looks back and forth, and each one of us thinks the exact same thing I just thought. Fuck.

We make quick work of setting up small cameras and tracking devices. Blade already has a shift worked out. The two of us take the first one, monitoring the building. The others head back to keep an eye on Kat. She's going to be pissed when she finds out we didn't tell her the details.

"One way or another, K-Love is going to realize this was the best way," I can't help saying the words out loud to Blade.

"Tank, we do need to talk about the future. I know Kat was involved in this because of a lot of her personal factors. In the future, for everyone's best interest, it is club business only."

"Agreed, brother. I don't want shit like this creeping up and biting us in the ass again. It could have ended a lot worse than it did."

Families make mistakes and feelings can alter the perception of truth. Never again will I let my feelings hold judgement over my club. I realize now how my personal feelings altered their lives, and it wasn't right to do that to them. There will always be two things I need to survive this life, my club brothers and my family with Kat.

CHAPTER 24

Kat

Days have gone by and my skin prickles because a storm is brewing, I can feel it. Tank and the guys have been gone on club business which means they have a lead and they aren't sharing.

I'm struggling with my demons from the past and jump to conclusions that Tank and the club are setting me up. But, with every passing moment, that gets more difficult. Between him and I, this doubt grows. At least it feels like that for me. And each day that passes with no information, the walls rebuild around my heart.

It's been a natural response for my entire life. Can I change? What I do know is that if I don't change, my son will learn these behaviors from me. I don't want that poison I've been taught to seep into his little soul.

Frustration runs through my body and I can't think straight anymore. I decide to take a break. When I get outside in the sun, I find Spider sitting on a bench, smoking. I hold my hand out and ask for one, and he passes me his pack along with a lighter. Sitting down next to him, I light one and pass them back to him. After an exhale, he asks, "You holding up okay?"

"Yes. I am okay." I take a drag because I don't want to elaborate further. Spider watches me though, and I know he sees it, but I try to hide it none the less.

"Kat, you and I are a lot alike. In the dark, we can hide and work where we feel the most comfortable. I get away with hiding in the dark. I know my place in the club and in life." He turns to me and points with his smoke between his fingers, "Kat, get out of the webs, live in the light. Let Tank take care of you. That's where you will be the happiest."

He stubs out his smoke, tossing it to the ground and stepping on it with his boot. He leaves me alone with his words. What the hell does that even mean? I've definitely entangled myself into a messy life with my choices along the way, but I also feel like I had to survive.

I need to clear my head. There is just too much, and, maybe after this is all over, I can concentrate on making things easier and lighter. Maybe, just maybe, I can have a more normal life. I'll keep fighting for the best things in life. It is time that I stopped running from the good.

After I finish my smoke, I stand to go back inside when a car pulls up. I freeze and my blood runs cold at the sight of a beaten and bruised Jane. She is sitting in the passenger seat, with a gun held to her head. One man is in the driver's seat and two are in the back, pointing the gun at her. The driver rolls the window down just enough for me to hear her, exposing only half of her face. She is alive. Just as fast, it hits me, I realize why. Matias has hurt her beyond healing.

"You have ten minutes to meet us at 310 South Street. If you don't, I die." The window is rolled up and I back away. I came out here with nothing to protect myself or her. I have no gun, knife, nothing. If I yell for Spider, they will speed away and, more than likely, shoot her.

There is only one thing I can do, go get her myself. I owe her that much.

Instead of going into the motel room where Spider is, I urgently walk into my own and arm myself with guns and knives. Grabbing the keys from the dresser, I step outside the door only to find Stryker blocking my path. "Kat, no. Not your fight, go back inside."

I try to push past him, ignoring his words because the anxiety claims my senses, wanting to get to Jane as fast as I can. Stryker's hands grip my shoulders, and before I know what is happening, I am spun around and back inside my room. The door slams shut behind me. I whip around, coming face to face with the MC Prez.

"They are going to kill her," I grit out the words between my teeth and my fists clench at my sides.

Stryker's arms cross over his chest. "They need you, Kat. If they have you, they will torture you and finally kill you after they have the information they need to prove that Matias didn't steal his own drugs and money from the other Cartel Bosses. You will slit all of our throats with one step out that door."

His face tilts to the side with the glare of a killer. "I love Tank like my son. If I have to kill you to keep my entire family safe, I will do it. Then I will have to kill Tank because he will come after me for hurting you." He pulls a nine-millimeter from his back and holds it at his side. "I want you to understand one more thing. I would have killed you already, but you are breathing because of him. What you know could kill each and every one of us. Do we understand each other?"

I understand perfectly well what he means. That he would have ordered the men to put a bullet between my eyes because I know what they did. I hold club secrets, and no one is to know those and live to tell the story.

Inhaling a breath is like breathing with broken ribs, the reality of this is that painful. "They hurt her, Stryker, because I failed to protect her," I painfully admit. "He more than likely raped her for hours, and his men did, too. Beat her and broke her bones to get the information they wanted." I don't know who I am pleading with, maybe the heavens to right these wrongs.

"We offered for them to stay with us. We couldn't hold them against their will to protect them when that would've put us at risk, and they didn't want our protection. Why should I put my men at risk? I am sorry for your loss, but you, as a leader, have to learn to minimize the risk for your family. You can't save everyone. You can't go back and save your sister over and over. She died."

My world shatters again at the truth he explains so freely. My chest heaves and I sit back on the bed with my head in my hands. "It never gets easier. Each body that lies in the wake of this dark world. Each soul that crosses over never makes any sense, and there is nothing at the end of it."

Stryker sits in the chair across from me. "You have seen more than most in this life. To make the decision of who lives or dies never feels right. But the why is easy. To protect my family, I will kill them all and wear the battle scars for them. Let Tank carry that burden for you. Free yourself of that pain."

My head raises and, once again, I see the Prez of the Battle Born MC, but this time, it is the leader and protector.

Tank

As soon as we heard that Matias had sent the men to the hotel address where we were staying at, Stryker called and said he had eyes on Kat and would text us with directions next. Now I'm pacing back and forth.

We knew from the bugs we placed that he wanted her alive. The only question is if she went rogue on me.

Spider live streamed the whole exchange outside of the motel, so we saw and heard everything they said. Thank God she hadn't been armed, who knows what she would have done.

Once we had the directions for the meet, we left for the location where he is now standing inside an abandoned bakery. Armed guards are at the doorway and they escort Jane in with shackled hands and feet. The asshole punches her in the face and breaks her nose before tying her to a chair. All for Kat's benefit when she shows up.

All this does is enrage me further to charge in there and beat the shit out of him myself with my own hands.

"You understand that Jane may not make it out of there alive?" Blade asks, and I know why. Once we get close enough, Matias will use her as a shield and that could sign her death warrant.

"To protect the club and Kat, I will do what I have to." I don't need to look at Blade to know that he gave the order for the men to start the next phase. Feet start to quietly move across the floor of the business we broke into to watch the building across from us.

Blade looks at his phone and confirms that we go in minus thirty seconds. He counts down and Saint and I hold out rifles with a steady aim. At the end of the count, we send the two front guards to hell with a bullet between the eyes. The brothers storm in from the back and front. Finally, the last battle to win the war has begun.

We leave our rifles and run across the street to help in the gun fight, taking out as many as possible on our way in. Running across the street, double fisting our handguns, we shoot anything that moves.

The building suddenly drops into dead silence. Slowly, we creep around the rooms and the dead bodies of the Cartel, until finally we reach the last room. Blade and Saint look at me from the other side of the doorway leading in.

"Katherine," Matias yells for her. "Come out and I'll let her go. You have ten seconds before I slit her throat. Come out now."

We look at each other because we know he will never let Jane go. She wails in pain and we hear his manic laughter filling the space. Not wasting another second, I step around the doorway and hold my gun, aiming for his head. Matias pulls the knife out from her leg and holds the bloody blade to her throat. "Where is she?" His darken voice makes Jane shake with fear.

"She's not here. Let her go, fight me."

He laughs more, "I have no use for you," he lies. The look in his eyes tells me that he knows exactly who I am. Within seconds, his pupils dilate, and the killer has chosen death. His hand grips the blade and he is ready to slit her throat as a distraction before he sends a bullet into me.

Mercy. I choose mercy for poor Jane and shoot her in the head. It snaps back and Matias' face is sprayed with blood. I duck and roll to the left before Saint sends a bullet into his arm that has the gun which was aimed at me. The weapon clatters to the ground and I jump up to take him down.

Pure adrenaline mixed with fury laces my blood, and all I see is red. My fists fly for his face, hitting him two times before he falls backward and to the floor. I follow, then attempt to jump back, but it's too late when his knife misses my torso, sticking into my thigh instead.

My hand covers his and my fist rears back and beats his face with two jabs. His grip loosens on the blade and I rip it out with a roar before plunging it into his arm, then tossing it to the side. His screams of pain ignite the animal within me, and my hands wrap around his throat. I wait for him while he struggles underneath me.

Leaning forward, my hands let up just enough before I kill him. I sadistically whisper, "You're not dying today, you sick fuck. You are going to the mine and only God knows how long you will last before your body will finally die."

My hands beg to be freed and finish this. Not today, though, not after everything he has done. My fists beat his face so many times it turns into mush and blood. Blade and Saint pull me back before I do finish him here. They tie his feet, then flip him over and zip-tie his hands together.

Together, they drag him up and he groans from his wounds. This smaller in stature man, he's minimal compared to my height and weight, and, just to hammer it home, I'm going to knock his fucking lights out.

First, I take my size thirteen boots and kick his stomach and ribs. I don't stop until he throws up, and I am sure he doesn't have not one rib that's not broken. My large fist punches that motherfucker square in the face while Blade and Saint hold him.

His head snaps back, just like how he did to Jane, but doesn't fall to the floor because of the support from my brothers. "Lights out, motherfucker, that was for Jane."

We load up two bodies in the van. One of them is sedated and the other is dead. We drive back to the motel to pack up and head out of Texas. It's like a hornets' nest with the brothers running around and packing up as quickly as possible. Everyone is ready to leave and we hit the road in record time.

Kat rides with me on the back of my bike back to Las Vegas where we stop after a long haul. We have a small ceremony for Jane at an unmarked grave. Kat doesn't know, but Stryker buried with her any evidence we could gather should it ever need to resurface. Also, a hard drive worth millions of dollars.

I hold Kat's hand as she says goodbye to her friend and the woman who protected Eli for us. Her questions still haunt me whenever I think of them.

"Tank, how did she die?" Her fingers run over the scabs on my knuckles. I just finished telling her the first half of the story we had kept away from her.

"I gave her mercy, K-Love," I answer for her honestly.

Her fingers still and she looks up at me, "You had no other option?"

My hand pushes the black silky strands of hair away from her face. "Baby, she would've probably never been normal after what she lived through. It was either me or him. I would have saved her if I could've."

Kat wraps her arms around my body and holds on tight. She may never understand or agree with my choice of killing Jane. But some choices aren't choices at all, and we will stand behind each other no matter what. Trust freely in those who hold your heart.

Maybe later, Stryker will need the money, but, right now, while things are still hot, it's best not to have that on any of us. He may use it for the club or to frame someone. That hard drive could be worth more than money, but life or death.

Before we tipped off the Cartel leaders where the drugs were stored, Cuervo made a run down to Mexico City and killed the guy, Cervantes, that Kat had blackmailed to work for her.

No loose ends.

Cuervo used his phone and sent a text with the location of the drugs and where he had hidden the money. Or should I say, where Cuervo planted some of the hard drives of cash for the Bosses to find. All is well in Cartel land.

The Bosses had actively looked for Matias until he was reported as shot and burned to nothing in Mexico City. It was Cervantes' body; Matias is actually tied up in the back of the van, on his way to the mines.

It's been a long ride back to Reno, and coming home never felt so good. Especially when we reach the mine. I get out and slam the car door shut and stretch, letting the sun heat my face. All is right in the world.

Matias is pulled by his ankles, in his blood-soaked Armani suit, out of the back of the vehicle and onto the ground. Cowboy's nose scrunches from the stench of him lying in the back of the van for two days straight.

"Cut his clothes off, tie him to that pole and hose him off," Blade orders and marches inside the mine.

Cowboy groans, "How are we going to do that?"

I scratch my beard because I have to agree, I don't want to touch the asshole either. After a few supplies are brought out from the building, we cut his pants and shirt off and toss them into a fire pit next to us. Matias doesn't fight while we remove everything off his body, but as soon as I get his hands tied and connected to the pulley, he screams in pain around the gag in his mouth.

Several large bruises cover his ribs and stomach. Cowboy turns the water on at full power from the utility hose. I spray his ribs first, chuckling as he squirms and screams in pain. I laugh at his discomfort and finish hosing off the little puke, leaving him hanging there to air dry.

Blade steps out from inside the mine and nods at me to take him into the building. When we release the binds that are holding him up, he slumps to the ground, breathing heavily. We pick him up by the arms and help to drag him into the room that was set up for him. He's shackled to a table by his hands and feet when we hear our next guest arriving.

We go outside only to see a large, disgusting, beastly looking man getting out from the truck that Spider brought him in. We point to the doors and the man smiles and walks into the building. It doesn't take that fat dirty fucker long to get to business. That piece of shit has a long rap sheet of raping boys and men in prison. A nobody in the grand scheme of things, but here to do a job. Spider offered him money to rape Matias, and, by the sounds of the horrendous screaming and grunting filling the air, it's more pleasure than a job for this sick fuck.

The four of us sit outside vigilantly for a few hours and some of the shit that is said by that man will haunt me for the rest of my life. We allow him a few rounds before we knock on the door, signaling that he is done. The fat fuck steps out of the building with a smile on his face. "Anytime you boys need help, you give big D a call." He says this while zipping up his bloody dick.

Spider's evil gleam doesn't even wait. He aims his pistol and shoots his brains out. We all take a breath that this disgusting piece of shit isn't on this earth anymore. We help roll up the body in plastic and Spider hauls him off to an unmarked grave, deep in the hills of Nevada, with Cowboy's help.

Blade and I walk inside, and I fight the gag that threatens to hit my throat at the condition Matias' ass was left in afterward. Blood coats the area and his back is scratched so badly, it bleeds in several places. Once Matias sees us, his eyes turn to stone.

"Fuck *you*. When I get out of here, I am going to kill all of you for years." With his gag removed and the blood that paints his mouth, it looks like he gave a blowjob, too.

"You think that you and your filthy bikers scare me? Wait, *cabrón*, until my men come looking for me and find me here. All of you are going to die," Matias threatens. It could be scary, and it probably was back when he had the full weight of the Cartel behind him.

I shrug at the tied-up man before me, "One. Everyone thinks you're dead. And two. If they didn't already, then they would be hunting to kill you themselves after all the drugs and money you stole." I cluck my tongue at him, "I bet I could sell you for a pretty penny, but I won't."

He holds still and realization sinks in, so he tries another tactic. "Katherine is one hot *puta*, *sí*? She loves to get fucked rough, doesn't she? You're welcome, *pendejo*. I sent her to get the information I needed on your club. She was my little *puta* spy."

Blade stares intently and I shrug as I'm trying to keep my cool. "You are right about that. She is one hot woman. Too bad your insults are bullshit. She's the one who tore you down. How does that make you feel? Your own wife basically raped you today. The woman you loved and gave all your secrets to. That shit has to burn like a motherfucker."

Matias' hands pull at the binds and screams, "Bring that *pinche cabrona* to me!"

"For what?" I laugh in his face, squatting down to meet him eye to eye. "I'm going home to her. She's mine, *pinche pendejo*, you'll never see her again."

I take a blow torch, turning it on high, and set his skin on fire. The back of his head becomes bald, missing all the hair now. His screams of agony don't phase me at all. Turning the torch off, I leave the fucker there for the night, and go home to my woman.

CHAPTER 25

Kat

To say I am nervous is an understatement. Finally, we got a hold of Fuego and he is on his way back with Eli. That is not what I am nervous about, though.

Tami.

I stare at her from across the room of her house. An empty home, void of love within its walls.

She didn't answer when I knocked. Tank nudged me from the back, and I glared at him when he shoved me forward through the door.

Tami turns and remains impassive, not happy, not mad and not sad, just nothing. "Hi," I lamely approach.

Tank bulldozes full speed ahead and picks her up from the chair. "Hey, little T." His gigantic arms hold her to him, and she breaks with a burst of affection. Cash is asleep in the bassinet next to her where she was reading during his nap.

"I didn't know if I would see you again," she sniffles into his chest.

"Girl, that is offensive. Of course no one will stop the big D.O.G. from coming home." She actually smiles just a tiny bit for him. That is before she notices me and her smile disappears.

I freeze on the spot because I don't know how she feels about me, and I am scared of how she will react. Tami lunges for me and, at first, I think that she will wrap her little hands around my throat, but she doesn't, she wraps her arms around me.

My own limp arms go up and I hug her back and whisper, "I am sorry, Tami. I hate that this happened, just so sorry."

"Shhhh. Kat, you didn't kill him," she chokes on her words.

"You kept Eli alive for me."

She pulls back and her teary eyes look into my own. "I would do anything for him and you. You are my family." When I don't say anything, she continues, "Kat, it is not your fault. You needed help. Stop being responsible for everyone. You have to stop that." Tami actually teases me even though her eyes betray her sadness and tears that get away.

"She really does, little T. I keep telling her, but goddamn, that woman," he points right at me, "Never listens to a fuckin thing I say." Cash starts crying from Tank's loud boisterous voice, and he bends over to pick up the growing baby. "Hey, tiny T, you missed me, too, didn't you, little dude?"

Cash calms down when he is held in his arms. "Kat, check out his baby tooth." Tank holds Cash out with both hands straight in front of him. Tami and I both laugh a little and Tank winks.

I realize right then what I'd missed before. Tank is this funny man because it is his way of coping somedays and wanting to bring happiness to the people he loves. If you looked close enough, you would see the pain in those handsome eyes with tiny sexy wrinkles around them. My Road Dog has many layers and all of them are good.

At first, I was pissed off when Stryker held me captive until it was time to leave. Then, I realized that it was not my place to be involved in their business even if it did involve me, too. Ultimately, their club was saving my life and I needed to learn what being humble and trusting really was.

Tank's words rang through in my mind, *"I will protect you, even from yourself,"* and they made sense when I sat across from Stryker and he said, *"Let Tank carry that burden for you. Free yourself of that pain."*

Tank knew all along how to handle things and his club. He protected me in Texas and took care of business. He continues to protect me now by saving me from my own doubts with Tami. He is my hero, my Road Dog for life.

We stay at Tami's for dinner and, even though I am exhausted, I am happy to cook for them, like old times. We watch stupid T.V. until a very tired Tami falls asleep on the couch. I cover her with a blanket and hold my keys in my hands, but it is strange the feeling I have. I am glued to the spot on the floor where I'm standing.

"You can't leave, can you?" Tank's warm hands slide around my stomach.

"No, I can't leave. I feel like I need to make sure she is okay. I know she's not. She is trying to be brave, but she is really broken in there, Tank."

His hands leave my waist, but he pulls me along with him to the spare room. He locks the door and stands mere feet away from me. "We will stay here tonight, but I need to feel you right now."

Slowly, I pull my shirt over my head and beg, "I need to feel you. I need you to make me feel alive without the hurt." I start removing all of my clothes while he watches and does the same. For the first time in my life, I crave the sweet and the soft. He can only bring this attachment from me this way. Only my Tank can.

Stepping backward to the bed, I never take my eyes off him. Tank continues removing his clothes, and by the time he reaches me at the bed, he is completely naked, with his glorious hard cock ready for me.

I spread my legs even wider for him. His eyes scan my entire body and stare at my pierced clit. "I fucking love your pussy. That diamond marks it as *'Property of Tank.'*" He growls and crouches before me.

I giggle at the possessive sound he makes. He bites the inside of my leg and I laugh out loud at his playfulness. He lays a sweet kiss on my pussy before saying, "Love you, Kit Kat."

He then goes in for a long lick. "Oh shit, I love you, too, baby."

He hums and keeps on laving me up until he asks, "You love this, too? My tongue on you making you need more?"

"Fuck yes, I love," I gasp when he sucks my ring and clit into his mouth, "You."

Tank doesn't stop and gives it to me soft, slow and sweet. This has become my favorite, and now I get why. It is so much more than the "O" that you get in the end, it is about connecting with each other. I let him lick and suck me until my back arches and my toes curl while I come from his time well spent on loving me.

Tank crawls up my body and my hands grab his face to bring his lips to mine. Tasting myself on his tongue. I appreciate his lips as much as he did mine before and devour him with my kiss.

My legs wrap around him and he moves until his cock slides in. His low moan vibrates through my chest. This is the single sexiest moment of my life. I hold on tightly with my legs, and my fingers run through his beard, neck and hair.

His thrusts are meaningful with every rock of his hips into me. Each one is meant to show me love and intimacy. I never want it to end, the comfort it brings is addicting. His hand comes up and he caresses my breasts and twists my nipples through his fingers, making my pussy clench around him.

He starts quickening his movements and pounds into me as my orgasm starts closing in. My hands claw into his biceps and hold onto him. I can't hold off when he pinches my nipples again. We go off together, sharing the orgasm and love between us. His lips find mine and kiss me goodnight before he wraps me up in his arms.

Tank gives me all of him and we find a little peace in each other to face another day together, never apart and never alone.

CHAPTER 26

Kat

Tank has been gone for a while. I suspect where he went and why, but I don't want to even know anything more than that. With some things, you reach a point where the details don't matter. The man I was married to before doesn't even mean anything to me anymore. Waking up today feels like a dawn to a new life. A fresh start at life with a man who deserves all the happiness that he gives.

Today feels like a thousand pounds have been lifted off my shoulders. Each step through the house feels lighter than the one before. I find the kitchen empty, but a pot of coffee has been made. I grab a cup and fill it before I go in search of Tami and I know exactly where to find her.

She is sitting in a rocking chair on her back patio, with a sleeping Cash in her arms. Next to her is an empty baby bottle and a coffee mug. I take a seat opposite her and look out to the beautiful sunrise. I close my eyes for just a moment. Freedom and victory warm my soul. I made it.

"Are you happy?" Tami tests, startling me from my daydreaming with the little bite to her tone. My eyes pop open and I turn to face her.

"Yes and no. It is a long story. If you want to hear it, I'll tell you about it. But I do want to hear about you and how *you* feel."

She thinks about my words for a moment and then tells me her truth. "I missed you and hated you at the same time for a while. My feelings were so extreme from one moment to the next that I'm glad I had time to think about them for a while before you came back."

I nod my head because I can't blame her at all. "Talk to me, Tami, if you need to. I can take it. I want to be here for you."

She rocks Cash while rubbing his back. He must be close to four months now, and I'm amazed at how much he grew while I was away.

Tami's eyes start watering. "You know what happened that day, and I would save Eli again if I needed to. It's that I couldn't save *him*. Solo died because of the war the MC had with the Cartel. I was angry at you for leaving Eli with us because, had you not, then Solo would have lived."

She wipes her tears with Cash's blanket. The guilt swarms around me but I sit and wait her out. I will listen to everything she has to tell me because it is the least I can do for her.

"I was angry at Solo for taking him outside to play because we were on lockdown. Cuervo held me back. What if he let me go and I was able to warn him? Axl didn't protect him like Solo did him. What if I didn't go out there to grab Eli, then maybe he wouldn't have been distracted?"

Tami's voice falters from the anguish living in her. "Kat, I blamed everyone and myself. But, in the last few months, I realized that it was because I was alone that I was so angry, and I didn't know how to deal with it. I could be angry at the world and it would never bring him back. The war started a long time ago whether you or the MC wanted it to or not."

I sit, stunned, wondering if at some point she still may not forgive me and what that would mean for us.

Tami looks out into the yard. "I knew what Solo did for a living when I got involved with him. He then became everything to me, and I forgot those things. We were invincible, had all these plans for a wedding and kids. It wasn't only Solo that died, it was my future as well. Now I need to live figuring out what my life is going to be like, alone with Cash."

"I am so very sorry, Tami, that your life changed. You know that, right? I wanted you to have the life I never got, a real second chance at something perfect."

Tami smiles just a little, not like she used to though. "I know you did. You took good care of me before. While you were gone, Harley stayed here right after, and helped me. She took care of me and Cash. She held me through the grief. She's been great, but I really missed you, too, I realized. I was angry that you weren't here."

My hand reaches out to squeeze hers. "I wanted to be here more than anything, too. I missed you and Cash like crazy and never stopped wondering if you were okay. A part of me was scared to come back. What if you didn't want to talk to me again?"

She chuckles a little and teases, "The Black Widow was scared?"

"She's dead, Tami. She died on the day Tank took on the world for her. He has been our hero. But Kat was scared, she's still scared. Tami, I love you like a sister. I don't want to lose you."

"We are okay. I love you, too, and I am happy you are home now."

"Are *you* okay?" I tentatively ask, wishing for a miracle.

"No. I am better, but far from okay."

The sliding door opens and Vegas, Dana, Harley, Jenn and Emilia step outside and greet us. Vegas is the first to wrap her arms around me, then followed by the rest. They bring in bags of food and sit with us.

Even though there has been so much loss, there has never been so much good either. Vegas' twin boys and little Maddison have their one-year-old birthdays coming up soon. They chase each other, crawling around the backyard, not interested in food anymore. If anyone could bring Tami back from heartbreak, it would be these ladies. I've never been more grateful for them.

Harley takes Cash from Tami and cradles him to her chest, kissing his sweet baby cheeks. Looks like he is the healing miracle. We sit around and tell stories of what happened while we were apart, leaving nothing left unsaid. Through the laughter and heartbreak, we put ourselves back together and strengthen our bond.

I'm in the middle of laughing at what Vegas and Dana did to one of the new prospects while they were on their house arrest when the door opens and my heart stops at the sight of my little angel.

"Eli," I call to him with my arms held open. He hesitates for a moment and my heart drops, wondering if he forgot me already. Something resonates though and he comes running into my arms. "Hey, baby boy, did you drive your *Tio* Fuego *loco, mijo?*"

"*Este niño,* that boy needs twenty-four-hour surveillance."

I chuckle while he slaps a wet kiss on my cheek. "I know, he's a lot better when Tank is around."

His little head whips around, looking for the big guy, and I feel bad he wasn't here when he came home, "Tank—"

"*Tu padre,*" Fuego's mother interrupts me. "I spent the last two months talking about his *madre* and *padre.* You are going to confuse the *niño pequeño.* It's about time you," she points a finger in my direction, "give that man the respect he deserves, *mija.* That's his *bebé,* too."

"*Sí, abuela.*" I swallow the rock in my throat. "*Tu papá volverá pronto*, your dad will be back soon, okay?" I sweep his feather soft hair away from his forehead.

"*Sí, madre*," he says, wiggling out of my grip when he notices the other kids playing in the yard. I put him down and he runs after them. When I stand up, I see the humor hiding in all their eyes, but I wait until after *abuela* walks over to love on her other great grandkids.

"How in the hell am I going to tell Tank he is now called *padre*?" I smack my own forehead and groan.

"I think he is going to love it," Jenn smiles. "Just be careful. He can take things overboard and, before you know it, he will get *you* into calling him Daddy. In which case, I never want to hear about it."

They all agree that yes, this will be the highlight of Tank's week and also my demise.

CHAPTER 27

Tank

We didn't want to have a memorial for Solo at the graveyard. He had meant so much to all of us. We hung a picture of the group of us in the garage and the bar. We toasted to the picture in the bar with beers in hand like he was sitting right there with us. We took turns telling stories and laughed about the fun times we all had.

His cut is in the safe for now. Blade still hasn't decided what he wanted to do with it at this point since there is evidence of his last few moments still alive on it. We all feel the void of him being gone. He had his place here in his own way, and now, there is nothing. Since we lost a brother, we had a special patch made and sewn onto our cuts. A single wing attached to an S.

The MC took a long ride around Lake Tahoe. We loaded onto our bikes and took a memory run to respect a fallen brother. I can't help but think of the irony of how many runs he went on by himself, and how, this time, it was a solo trip into the next life.

We rode for about an hour and the brothers went back to the club while Blade and I dropped down from Tahoe into Carson City, then straight to see Pawn.

Blade stays outside to wait for me. I think he knows that I need to see Pawn alone.

After the guards let me in, I wait for him to join me at a table. His stride seems a little slower than normal when he finally walks in.

"How are you holding up, brother?" There are some bruises that have faded into an ugly orange around his cheekbone and he has a small cut above his eye.

"It's been rough but nothing I can't handle." Pawn self-consciously runs a hand over the cut and sits back in his seat. "Did everything get settled at home?" Meaning, did we get Matias.

"Yeah, everything has worked out." I rap my knuckles on the table. "We are behind you all the way, Pawn. We all feel the loss with you and now with Solo leaving us. I feel responsible for this mess. I am supposed to be the big dog of our pack and I failed my brothers."

"Don't," Pawn interrupts. "I put myself here because of my choices. I fucked her and made Cash, and didn't see the setup. Solo tried to get me to leave and I didn't listen to him." His head hangs before looking up again. "If I hadn't been stupid and had listened, he might still be alive because I would have been there to have his back."

He looks away, shaking his head like he's trying to make up his mind. I know what he's thinking right now, and, in all the months he's been here, he never asked the question. Until now.

"Has she sent anything?" I think he needs to hear from her that she is okay. But I have to give him the truth.

"No. It's been rough on her. She was there when it happened, and she stayed with him until his last breath. She saved Eli, and Solo saved Axl, and, in the end, Solo gave us everything." Pawn intently listens to every word and looks down in understanding.

"You would say to us, '*We aren't born until we battle.*' Don't leave Tami alone. Watch over Cash for me, yeah?"

"Always and forever, brother, they are my family. We'll keep them safe. Why don't you write to her, let her see you?"

He shakes his head, "I don't want her here. This is no place for her or Cash. Makes shit harder for me seeing them, would give me hope." He stands and lifts his chin, "Thanks for coming."

"Remember what I taught you, hit them with that left uppercut you got."

He takes a few steps back but keeps his eyes on something behind me. Standing, I turn to my left to walk out and see a large dude watching my movements. Outside the doors stands a guard we put on our payroll to help keep tabs on Pawn while on lockup. The door shuts and, as I walk by, I say, "The Black Rose, Friday night, twelve midnight"

He hands me my cell and wallet, "Have a nice day," and gives me an affirmative nod.

What the hell is happening now?

Blade, who waited for me by our bikes, stomps out a smoke as soon as he sees me walking out. "We have a meeting at the Black Rose tomorrow night with Blackbird." Which is the guard's codename, we never use his real name. "Someone is putting the beating on Pawn and we need to find out why."

"Fuck, Tank, when will this shit settle?" Blade answers while swinging a leg over his bike.

"With our business, I'm guessing never." I sit on my bike, and, before I crank it on, I throw out one more thought. "I'm beginning to think that we were the suckers to take over this territory and your old man made the job of the Prez look like a keg stand."

"Say fucking what again?"

"A keg stand, like a cake walk." I shrug and put my helmet on, then crank my girl on. Blade's laughter is barely heard over the noise, and he signals with a finger to head out. The Prez and the Road Captain take the road back home to the clubhouse. One task done but my day is far from over.

At the clubhouse, I grab the rock crawler truck and throw in the back some rope, wood, screws and a camera with a battery pack. "I think that's about it." I pull the ties down tightly against the wood for the journey and toss the screws into the truck along with a drill.

"What's that about?" Axl asks, walking out from the garage.

"I'm doing a little construction up at the mine. Matias needs to see what it is like to be cornered. You coming?"

"Hell yeah, I'm in." Axl jumps in the front passenger seat and I drive us up there. We take the long run through the mountains.

Axl holds on to the handle and I hit the gas to propel us over a small hill, with sagebrush scraping under the truck. He hollers, "Motherfuckin' asshole!" Our heads almost hit the roof and we come down with the truck bouncing off the ground. We skid left, then right before I gain control of the vehicle.

I speed ahead on the open floor of the desert and find a sand dune. "Hell yeah!" I yell and stomp on the gas, making a hard-left turn and spinning the truck around a few times before we race out of there and find more mountains to jump.

An hour later, we reach the mine and jump out to unload our supplies, pumped after an afternoon of adrenaline rushing through our veins. Axl holds two boards for me after I put them together. One is about six feet long and the other is two. I continue handing them to him and I screw the open box together, whistling along to the radio I left on inside the truck to drown out the hollering from Matias inside.

The sun beats down on us like a torch. I rip off my shirt to wipe the sweat from my face and toss it aside to look over my work. "Okay, looks good. Help me get the asshole into the box."

We walk into the mine and find Matias still tied to the table where we left him. Axl takes a knife from the truck and cuts the rope.

He's so weak that he is barely able to move from his spot. Handing my knife to Axl, I step forward. Matias springs to life with whatever energy he had left to survive. He swings for my face and I dodge his fist and the next. My fist flies from the right and hit his nose.

Blood splatters and he snarls, coming for me again. I don't give him a chance and take the little puke down. This time, I punch and jab until he falls to the floor. I kick the same bruises over and over, and he yells in pain when my boot connects with his head. It falls to his side and his body relaxes from being knocked out.

I grip the two pieces of rope still tied around his ankles and pull him out the front door. His head bounces off the steps and his body leaves a trail of blood in the dirt.

Axl picks up his arms and we drop him inside the box. I then screw the lid down tightly after placing a small camera by his feet.

How do you torture a man who loves to use his mind as a weapon? You leave him alone to himself, with no one to communicate with. We pick up the box and tie it down in the back of the truck and hit the hills again, hollering like teenagers.

I don't miss every opportunity I can find to jump the truck. I grin at Axl when we take flight again and the back end hits hard.

"Blade is going to beat your ass when you get this back." He knows that we will fix it. We find the spot we had dug out on our way up here and finish what we came up here to do.

Occasionally, over the next several days, Matias screams or talks to himself. Driving himself mad with his own thoughts. He is missing fingernails from trying to claw his way out of the box, or rather the coffin I built for him with my own hands.

Matias has been buried alive and left alone in the desert so deep that not even the coyotes can get to him. But they can smell him. I sit on the mountain top and watch them circle around the spot. Only Axl and I know where that is. I'm betting that, since he rests in Native Tribal Land, it will be centuries before anyone could possibly come across it, if ever.

There is a small tube that feeds him water and another for oxygen. If he stopped drinking the water, he would die sooner, but his body refuses to let go of the basic necessity to survive. Some things are not worth your time, and he is something I never want to lay my eyes on ever again.

A Cursed King to the death.

CHAPTER 28

Kat

"I figured something out," Tank announces while holding a sleeping Eli in his arms. He fits perfectly snuggled up into his body and his little mouth hangs open. Protected, just like he should be.

As soon as Tank arrived home earlier, he gave me a quick kiss and hug. Then, they played so hard together, for hours, reuniting and picking up where the two of them had left off. Now, Tank has a serious face on that he doesn't wear often. So, I know this must be important to him.

"Why does Eli have my same name, *Lucas*?" His eyebrows scrunch together, creating wrinkles between them.

Nervousness takes over and I hesitate to tell him the truth, but I can't hide in the darkness anymore either. I pat the space next to me, and carefully explain. "After we hooked up for the first time here in Reno, I had your name added to his birth certificate. If I died, for some reason I just knew you would eventually find him." I bite my lip. "I wanted him hidden from his father, and the best way to do that was through you."

Tank sits down next to me, with a still resting Eli on his chest. "I blew it with my scene at the car crash." He heaves out a long breath. "He looked up everything about me and found him that way, and that led to who submitted the paperwork, didn't it?" His eyebrows raise, relaxing his features a little.

"Probably," I agree with him and rub his bicep. "I had already figured out that you had found Eli before, when you went away for a while. So, I was betting that, if something bad were to happen to me, you would look harder into his name."

"Lucas was another clue you had for me." His eyes move back and forth as a thought takes root, "You're now *Emily Scott*, though. What happened to Eli's mother on paper?"

Tank's confused face makes me smile and I just stare at him. I know that he will figure it out, and, after a few failed guesses, he's finally got it. "*You* died, didn't you?"

"Yes and no. Technically, I killed a woman named Hillary *Taylor*. She was written down as his biological mother and you as his father. Eli could never have my real name attached to him. Even though he's gone now, Matias had many enemies, and still may want to come after Eli for revenge."

"Whaaaat? Like, he's all *mine* and not yours for real?"

"Yes, he is *your* son and not mine. On paper," I make sure to point out. "Funny, isn't it?"

"Can I wake him up to tell him?"

My hand shoots out and I cover his mouth, "Don't you fucking dare. I am so damn tired; this kid never stops moving."

I feel Tank's big toothy grin stretching under my hand, and his eyes alight with mischief. Before I know what is happening, he is up and out of the room, then comes back without Eli and with the phone to his ear.

"Dana, I'm a baby daddy, like, for real!" He stalls a moment, then answers, "Wait, you said that he called me *padre* earlier and I missed it?"

Tank glares at me from his spot by the doorway, and I raise an eyebrow in response. "Oh, *abuela* taught him to call me *padre*. That doesn't feel right, though, we need to change it to *dad*." He goes back to what Dana is saying, whatever she's feeding his ego with on her end. "He's really mine! Kat put my name on the birth certificate after we boned in Las Vegas. So, I'm a legit baby daddy."

This could go on for hours and I miss him badly. I walk over to him and pull the phone away from Tank's grip and say goodbye to Dana before disconnecting the call. "You can tell everyone about being a baby daddy later. I miss you and want you to myself for a bit."

There is a knock at the door, and I squint my eyes at him. "What in the world are you up to?"

He smirks and shakes his head at me on the way to open the door for Harley, who's standing on the other side, smiling. "Hey, Kat," she walks in and drops her purse on the couch. "Aren't you guys headed out?" She looks between the two of us.

The confusion must be written clearly across my face. "We are?" I ask and turn to Tank.

"Yes, we are. Go get ready, I want you all to myself, too," he answers for me. Harley beams at us both, and her happiness starts to make me uncomfortable, like she knows more than me and that is not how this is supposed to be, not by a long shot.

I walk away from the room, but creep back around the corner and hide a bit to see if I can get some intel from them.

"Ms. Emily Scott, go get your riding gear on and quit hiding in the shadows, woman," Tank booms from the other room to me.

Peeking around the corner, I glare at Tank's humorous face. "You," he points at my face, "Need to start acting like a normal woman and get ready."

"I think eaves dropping is pretty normal for a woman," Harley snickers.

"Hurry up. *Emily*," he teases.

"Cool it with the 'Emily', *Road Dog*," I threaten and stomp off to the room, even though the new names are a little fun.

After I slide my boots and a jacket on, I tie my hair up, and go back only to find Tank and Harley chatting where I left them. I freeze and my nerves hit me hard. I've never been free to walk out the door. To live a life that belongs to me and just me alone.

These next few steps are different than before, and it feels like I am suddenly someone else. Tank sees my hesitation at the doorway and, thankfully, doesn't make a big deal about it. Instead, he grabs his wallet and keys from the mantel, then walks over to me and softly takes my hand in his.

"We'll be back in a while." He waves goodbye to Harley and I follow his lead out the door, to his bike in the driveway. "What is it, K-Love?" He gently glides his touch over my skin under my chin and lifts my face to meet his.

I swallow the golf ball lodged in my throat and take a moment to think about what it is that I am feeling. "I've seen hell and all the bad in the world. I lived with my father and I lived through the Cartel. What I have never experienced is whatever *this* is," I wave my hand to the world in front of me.

"Freedom," Tank rasps in understanding.

"Yes. Freedom," my lower lip quivers. "I have never in my life been free."

He lets go of a long exhale. "It is going to be a new start, a second chance at life. You'll see sunny days, and you'll see the hard ones, too. I'll protect you from the really bad ones. They are all waiting for you, Kat. There are no more games and no more fighting. You're free, baby."

A faint smile creeps up as I look into the face of my future. The eyes of the man who set me free and gave me the world. My hand covers his. "I don't ever want to be free from *you*. I want us forever."

"Baby, I will fight for you forever. You were meant to be free." This sweet man leans in to give me a soft reassuring, under the stars, that we were always meant to be, long kiss.

"Fly away with me, K-Love?" Tank gently tugs me over to his bike and I get on behind him. I hold onto him with everything that is *me*. As we cruise the road, every memory from the last few years surfaces. Flashbacks come, threatening to take me away, but Tank's hold on me is stronger.

I remember every hurt and pain and set them all free. The wind takes them away to be discarded. With every mile we ride, I get lighter and lighter. And the man driving this bike makes so much more sense to me now. The road is his healer and he needed me with him as much as I needed it.

Something spiritual happened to us along the way on our journey, that I don't know if I will ever fully understand. Maybe because we were stripped down to our bare souls that we found each other on the open road, and they fused together completely.

I do know this, though, our paths were always meant to be. We were made to travel them together. Tank will be my Road Captain for life. What will be, will be. I give him all of me, all of my submission. Most of all, I want to give him the world by doing just that.

Tank

Kat will always put on a brave face for those she loves. But I see the hurt hiding behind those eyes. It's been a hell of a ride these past few years. With a lot of pain and bullshit. I wanted her to feel the forgiveness of the road.

We needed to find some peace with our choices. A little distance in any blurry situation gives you some perspective. I called Harley before I came home and asked if she could watch Eli for us so we could ride together.

As soon as Kat walked back out from the bedroom, she looked lost in a world she used to dominate. It will take some time before she figures out who she is without the influences of other people forcing decisions from her. I can't wait to see her grow into her new role as a full-time mother.

The speed of the bike rips off the weights and chains of the world that have dragged us down. I know she feels it because, during our ride, her touch gets lighter with every mile. Kat is practically flying with me down the open road.

I think about Pawn, Solo and everyone who we lost along the way. The wind howls in my face. My heart bleeds out the regret of what could have been and what could possibly be. I picture letting go of it all, like it is a real thing, and let my mind roam free. Instead of the hurt, I start thinking of the possibilities. What can I do for my family?

This is why you only put your woman on the back of your bike. Stryker and Mad Max taught us this as young men. The road is our place of reckoning, our time for penitence. You don't share that with just anyone. The woman you want to share your journey with, only *she* rides with you.

My hand lets go of the handlebar and wraps around her calf. Kat feels me and her hand slides up my arm to hold onto my bicep. Connected as one on this newfound freedom and world, together, fighting for forever.

A few hours pass before the bad is purged and the time feels right. I turn the bike around and head over to the tattoo shop where I park out front. Kat gets off before me and sets her helmet on her seat.

She glances around the empty lot and follows me inside after I unlock the front door and flip on the lights. The front counter and furniture have a light coating of dust since we had to close up while we dealt with club business. Taking her hand, I lead her over to my workstation.

Opening a drawer, I pull out the drawing of a wolf and hand it to her. "I knew the first moment I saw you in Vegas that I wanted you. I looked for you for a whole year after that and kept on going back to that bar where we met. Even paid that bartender to call me if you ever returned there."

Kat's eyes round in surprise and I continue my confession. "I could never let you go either. Ever. Right before I saw you again, I swore it felt that I was going to find you. Then, when I did, at the motel, I knew you would never leave me again. We've waited, Kat, until our timing was right. I think that is today. Will you wear my brand?"

Her eyes sparkle from unshed tears. "I would love to." She uses one hand to wipe at her eyes and the other holds onto the wolf face drawn on the paper. *Battle Born* arches over the top and a simple *Tank* is stamped at the bottom. She goes to hand me the drawing back after carefully inspecting it.

I drop to one knee and pull out a diamond ring, sliding it onto her finger. "Ms. Emily Scott, will you marry me?"

Kat coughs and laughs, "You had to say that didn't you?"

"Well, that is the woman I am marrying," I smart back.

"Yes, Road Dog, I will marry you."

I kiss her hand and stand, pulling her into my body. "I can't wait to get this on you. Turn around and sit down in the chair. Take off your jacket and shirt."

Kat raises an eyebrow and does as I ask with her back to me. I clean and prep her neck before placing the stencil on her skin. The drawing covers the middle of her shoulder blades, peeking up her neck, and it looks perfect. Everyone will know she's my life.

I start the outline first and I don't get very far before she murmurs, "I love you."

CHAPTER 29

Tank

"Mmmm," I moan, pulling my stiff cock from her pussy after a few more pumps. I grit out, "Roll over onto your back, K-Love."

Finally, I got my woman right where I wanted her, naked and in our bedroom. Kat turns over and her tits bounce from her tossing herself back on the bed. She spreads her legs wide.

Pulling out a chain with nipple clamps on each end, I lay it across her ribs and bend forward, taking her nipples deep into my mouth. My teeth graze across her sensitive tips, and she gasps on each scrape over them. I twist one nipple with my fingers, getting the little fucker real perky before I place one clamp to it. She moans in pleasure because my girl loves this shit. I do the same to the other one and Kat wiggles her ass underneath me, searching for me, wanting me to give her a release of pure passion.

"Fuck my pussy hard, Tank," she gasps, begging for more dick.

I give the chain a light tug and her hands come up, cupping her breasts. On my way down her stomach, I trail kisses down to her pussy. My tongue snakes out to drive her clit wild with long strokes before giving her hard and fast ones and bringing her to the brink of ecstasy.

Her hands fall to the sides when I pull away right before she comes undone. She growls in frustration and I tug the chain a few more times. "You'll come when I want you to. Be a good girl and pull your knees up to your chest."

She takes her knees up and holds them tight to her. I slap her pussy lightly and she shivers from the lighter touch. I try it again but this time a little harder than the last. She squirms again and her chest heaves with desire.

"You looking for my cock to fill this pussy?" I taunt her and tug on the chain before I slap her wet cunt.

Her head falls to the side when I lean forward and lick her hard-pebbled nipples. I slip a small vibrator onto my thumb before pushing my cock back into her wet and silky heat. "Fuck, woman, I love this pussy."

I pull up onto my knees and turn the little vibrator on. "Come on my dick, baby, I want to feel you."

It takes all I have in me not to hammer into her silky tight cunt and blow my load. I hold back because watching her and feeling her is next level. Occasionally, I tug the chain and her breathing goes labored with every effort. My girl looks like a sexy goddess from heaven.

She holds onto her knees like I asked, and her body starts contracting around my dick.

"That's it, Kat, be my dirty girl, baby. Come on this cock, soak me."

She lets go, her orgasm squeezing the shit out of my cock, and I have to shut my eyes and breathe through it before I allow myself to let my own orgasm rip out of me. As soon as she comes down and relaxes a bit, I am ready to pound another one out of her.

I toss the vibrator to the side and grip her waist, then rear back and in again. I'm losing control with each thrust, fucking her as hard as she can take, which is all of me. So fucking close, but I need her with me. With every thrust, I pull on the chain. Her panting picks back up and I'm four thrusts from blowing my load. One more hard pull and then I rip the chain away from her nipples.

Kat's entire body shakes underneath me, and her pussy convulses, squeezing the hell out of my dick. Her mouth opens to scream out her pleasure, and I fall forward, covering it with my hand while Kat mumbles, "Oh. My. God."

I'm coming and laughing at the same time, "Babe, you can't wake the kid." A few more satisfying thrusts later and I pull out, then lie down next to her unmoving, sated body.

"That was— I just don't have the words," her head shakes from side to side. "I've never understood seeing stars, but, no shit, I am seeing those stars now."

"I would offer you a smoke," I pat my bare chest, "But I don't have any on me." I look around like they could pop out of nowhere.

Kat chuckles, and her hand stops me and my theatrics, "Fucking grade A, baby. Grade fucking A." She snuggles into me and I kiss her forehead.

"I have to go to work," I regretfully inform her. "I'll be back later tonight." I give her a light squeeze, wishing I didn't have to leave and that I could fall asleep with her right now. Rolling out of the bed my feet hit the cool floor and I head toward the bathroom to shower before I have to head out.

Kat is dressing and I don't think much of it as I'm drying off, until I see that she's putting her jeans on. "Ah, Kit Kat, where are you going?"

"I'll go with you to the bar and wait until you're done," she absently says while pulling her socks on.

"You're forgetting something—"

"Tank, don't ruin this night, please?" Kat cuts me off, "I just want to ride with you. I promise I won't even carry my gun, okay?"

Chuckling at her, I manage to get out, "No, babe, you could come with me, but you can't. There's a two-year-old boy we live with named Eli who is currently sleeping in the room next door," I point at the wall. "You can't take our baby on a ride along," I laugh at her and my chest shakes.

Kat falls back onto the bed and deflates, "I can't do shit anymore, can I? So, this is what it's going to be like from now on, isn't it?"

"Afraid so, you got what you asked for."

She shakes her head back and forth again, and I inform her while stuffing my keys, wallet and phone into my jeans, "Just wait until you have another baby." I start running out the door, yelling behind me, "Are you even on birth control?" and slam the bedroom door behind me. There is a loud thud that sounds behind it and my money is on that her boot hit it.

Life is just where I want it. If Kat isn't on birth control, I would love to see her pregnant with my baby. If she is, we'll have to fight over when she's getting off it. I'm ready for another baby and the thought of watching her grow with it makes me very possessive and happy. It's gonna happen, and soon.

Sitting at the bar at The Black Rose, I wait for the guard from the prison to show up after his shift. I snicker while taking a drink and thinking about the fit that Kat had before I left.

"What's so funny?" Spider slides into the stool next to me on my right.

"Earlier, before I left, Kat was pissed because she had to stay home."

Spider gives me a "what the hell" face and reaches over the bar to grab a beer from a tub of ice, then sits back onto his stool and pops the cap off himself, tossing a five on the bar top.

"She has to stay home with Eli now. I can't tell you how funny it was when she remembered that she was about to leave him home alone, and how mad she is that I get to go out without her and shake up the world now. Epic, bro. She is trapped in her own web and can't do shit about it."

Spider snickers while sipping his beer and looks around the bar full of people. He seems impassive before finally commenting, "I'm happy, Tank, that you two have everything worked out." He holds up his beer to me and then takes another long drink before setting it down.

Fuck, not now, Satan. I need another problem like I need a bullet in the head. "What is it, bro? Jazz still blowing you off? You need some help, or what is going on?"

"Nothing can be done. I fucked up and she isn't handing out second chances." I'm about to call bullshit but the door swings open and in walks our Blackbird. He spots Spider and I, takes the empty seat to my left and orders a beer, then gets straight to business without waiting on us to ask.

"Pawn isn't telling me much in there. He has eyes on him. A lot of the men in lock-up owed the Prez of the MC before you guys came in and took over. It's going to be a rough stent for him. He's not in a good spot with more of them in there."

"What other MC's or gangs inside can we hook him up with? I need some names to call favors in, now," I demand.

The guard nods and takes a chug, "I'll pull some of their enemies and call you with a list." He gets up from the chair and leaves the bar without another word or glance.

Running my hands through my hair, I notice Spider looking off into the distance before he turns to me. "Blade is waiting for us in the tattoo shop, with Axl."

I would say this isn't good because the four of us meeting under the radar is never a good thing. I nod in acknowledgment, and we both stand up and walk over. Once we are inside the shop and the door closes behind us, Blade hands me a folder. "Blackbird have any information for you?"

I hold the folder and tell him the status on where we are at, and he seems satisfied. He scratches his chin, a nervous habit he has, not often, but definitely his tell.

"Tank," he huffs and rests his hands on his sides, "We have some intel in that folder that we have to show you. I asked Spider to look up the information on who was handling the Cartel money in the States. It took him a few weeks to trace it back, but his findings are inside."

"Are you talking about the money we stole from the Cartel? You tracked down the guy before he tracked *us* down?"

"Yes, you know what happens next."

"A bullet to the head, no loose ends," I agree.

"Open it up, brother," Axl grimaces and I open the folder to find pictures of my father, on the street in downtown L.A., with a cell phone to his ear.

"What the fuck are you guys saying?" I can't stop myself from looking through the pictures of my dad meeting with marked men in the business.

"Are you kidding me right now? This makes no sense!" I drop my hands and look up at Blade, Axl and Spider, waiting for one of them to help me understand this better.

Spider steps forward. "Your father used the winery that he had bought as a front for his actual business. These big Bosses would bank their money with him, in his business, as investors, and he would clean up their accounts. We essentially stole money right out from under your father's nose."

Blade lights a smoke and inhales. "Stryker already ordered it to be done. He is the closest to Fuego, but wanted us to give you a heads up, and, possibly, dibs?" he asks, then releases the smoke.

Can I kill my own father?

CHAPTER 30

Kat

"What is the matter with the Road Dog?"

Tank's body is slumped over his coffee mug as he stirs the steaming liquid around in an endless circle, deeply lost into his thoughts.

He glances up at me from his task on the other side of the kitchen counter. When I set my mug down, he startles, coming out of the dark place he was in. "You are the perfect person to talk to about this." He turns in his chair to face me better from his spot next to Eli at the breakfast bar. "We need some family team building right now."

"Oh yeah? How am I the most perfect person to talk to, other than the obvious?"

Eli eats the last of his Cheerios and slams his hand down on the highchair table, demanding more food. Tank hands him a small handful from the box and I settle into the counter behind me, leaning back against it, waiting for him to continue.

"My dad was the one who was laundering money for the Cartel up here. *He* was the one paying off Johnny, the dirty MC members, the now dead casino guy, all of them. The money we took to frame that one guy, you know, your dead ex, was from the offshore accounts that *he* set up."

"Hmm, I guess I *would* be an expert on this one," I lightly laugh and take a sip from my coffee mug. "Now they want your father dead to clear up any possible leaks. Makes sense. What do you think about that?"

"It bothers me, K-Love, he is my dad. I thought that he left me because of the MC. But why, when he was a crooked mother— *jerk* himself?" Tank's almost mess up is damn cute.

"I would guess that he didn't want the MC to ultimately know his business and wanted you to help him in the long run. These men don't always play nice together. I bet he knew that the man that shall never be mentioned—"

"Thank you, babe."

"You're welcome. That he had bad blood with your MC and your father had to make a choice, you or the business."

"Obviously he chose his business." His sad little face pouts a bit.

"Tank, from my experience, these guys value money over people. Can you trust a man that left you behind *not* to come after the MC now? Will he protect you *and* the club? My whole entire family is dead because greed was more important to them than the love for each other. Go see your father, but my guess is, you already know what needs to be done. Quit talking yourself out of it."

Tank ignores my comments and starts talking to Eli, "You can't kill your daddy when you grow up because we are the bomb, the B's of life, baby E. We have a lot of adventure ahead of us, and a lot of team building."

After Tank's done chatting with baby E, I help him pack his bags for the road trip. "Burner phone, battery charger, two handguns and two extra clips. I tucked in two knives and my favorite tracking bug." I then rummage through his bags to make sure he has everything he needs. "It's all here, check."

Satisfied, I turn around and see Tank holding a stack of clothes and two pairs of socks. "Don't worry, I got my clothes. You will be the best housewife, Emily Scott, can't wait to marry you," he deadpans and tosses his clean laundry onto the bed.

"Damn straight, those worn out socks," I point right at them, "Aren't gonna do shit for you in a gun fight. You're welcome, Road Dog."

He smacks my ass on his way past me and asks, "What are you going to do for the next few days?"

"Try and do normal stuff. This house needs more furniture and whatever. I'm going to do the desperate housewife thing and spend all of the money while you are gone."

"And plan a wedding, too?" he jokes as he's tightly rolling and then packing his clothes into the small bag.

"No, we can elope or go to the courthouse or mail papers in. No wedding. And I am as serious as that loaded nine-millimeter in your bag. Just hell no."

"Whatever K-Love wants, she gets. Just don't shoot, woman." He holds his hands up in surrender, mocking me, before he grabs the bag on his way out.

Eli and I walk him out to the driveway, and we give him hugs and kisses before he is ready to take off.

"Say *bye, daddy*," I help Eli hold his little hand up and wave to Tank. He yells bye and giggles hard when Tank revs his engine for him on his way by. "Freaking boys, come on, *niño*, let's go see your auntie T."

We walk into the house and I load Eli up into the stroller, then remember that he needs snacks and drinks. I even pack an extra pair of clothes in the bag. It feels like something is still missing, though, and then it dawns on me that I need my gun. Reaching over, I pull open my nightstand drawer and grab the small handgun.

Unzipping the back compartment of the backpack, as I'm stuffing it inside, I halt all movement. "What am I doing?" I ask Eli and take the gun out, grabbing the other one with an extra clip. "There we go," and pack both of them, feeling better about having extra bullets with me. You never know, you know?

With the bag draped over the stroller, I'm ready, and I push him through the house, ready to go. Pulling the door shut behind us, I stop and look around the quiet neighborhood. The sounds of kids playing off into the distance, that's what I hear first. Then, I see moms driving by in their cars. It is a pretty normal Tuesday. I've never known what this looked like. A real mom. *Who* is that woman and *what* does she do?

My aching heart forces me to clench my eyes shut when I think about my own mother up in heaven. What she was like and the things that she would do with us when I was little. Some things will never be okay. Missing her will always be one of those things. Lately, letting things go or tucking them away has been difficult for me. Maybe because Eli and Tank have opened up my heart to a world I never had lived in before.

Thoughts of my mother stick with me on my walk, the memories of her. After several blocks, I find a park and stop to let Eli out to play. He excitedly runs to the little playhouse and immediately goes inside, exploring everything in there.

I take out my phone and snap several pictures of him, then send a few to Tank. Even though it makes me a little nervous, I talk myself into taking a picture with Eli and send that, too. It's been a long time since my picture was taken. Always hiding your identity will do that to you.

I sit on a nearby bench from where I can watch Eli run around the park, throwing whatever he can get his hands on up in the air. His joy and enthusiasm are a wrecking ball against any defenses I've had built around me before. This little guy shreds me. His emotions bring me to my knees.

Eli also makes me miss *her*, my mother, because of his affection. Would she love me, or *did* she love me like I do him? Would she love me now unconditionally like he does me? I know that she did.

"I'm sorry, momma. So sorry for all that I have done," I whisper quietly, hoping that my words reach her. "I did so many dark things. The one I hate the most was hurting Korina. I hope you forgive me."

It's like the air around me changes and I can feel her warmth. Her. My mom comes to me again. Maybe it was my conversation with Tank this morning that brought all these thoughts back, but it feels as if she is sitting here with me. She brings me peace, and I feel forgiveness, even though I don't understand why she would.

My words are caught in my throat. I never realized how much that was bothering me. I was so focused on being strong that I never saw the damage some of my choices had done to me. Everything we do has a consequence, mine is the pain and remembrance of living after their death.

I'm not sure how long I sit here and replay the memories in my mind. I question if I could have done things differently, and I still don't see how I could have.

"I have to let them go so I can be free," I murmur to the wind. Letting go is never easy and I want to be ready to do that. "I loved you, Papa and Korina. When we were kids. That is who I miss, the family we once were."

My mother adored my father at one time. I wonder what it had been like for her. What she went through before the end of it all.

The little girl in me is ready to be carefree and, like the breeze, I let these feelings drift away. I protected her for so long, the young girl I once was, but it's time to let her go too. She is strong enough to stand on her own. I mourn the loss of the family I never could before.

Eli comes running to me with his little arms wide open. He's finally worn out because he jumps up into my lap and snuggles into me. I embrace the tiny gift of life and love. He's my little treasure that no amount of money could ever replace.

I buckle him back into the stroller and, by the time I walk another block, he is quietly passed out.

My next steps are clear, they heal me so that I can love my family and not make the mistakes of the past.

CHAPTER 31

Tank

I met with Axl at the clubhouse, where we exchanged our bikes for an SUV. He came with me on the worst ride of my life, it feels like. Never in all my wildest dreams, and there have been some wild ones, did I ever think that I would be the one to put a bullet in my old man's back. As a kid, my dad came across as this smart and sophisticated businessman. After being in the MC for so long, I now know that the world is all smoke and mirrors.

I never looked for monsters in my own house, not at all. The day he told me I was as good as dead to him is still crystal clear in my head, like it all happened yesterday.

"What the hell do you mean, you are still riding with that garbage motorcycle club?" My dad pushes me back with his hand to my shoulder. He is a large man, like me, but I'm bigger. What his fucking problem with me is, I have no idea.

"I'm doing your classes for business, like you asked, chill out." I hold my ground, though, and step away from him at the entryway of my apartment. I'm sick of seeing him and of this same argument every time I've seen him since he found out who I was prospecting for.

His hand comes down on my shoulder, whipping me around to face him, with his finger in my face. "We have better things to do with your future. We are moving to California, there are more business opportunities there. Get rid of them by the time you graduate. You're moving and coming with us."

I laugh in his face, "I don't have to leave Nevada and I'm sure as fuck not living in California and working for you." The last few months of these fights have cemented that in my head.

"Oh, so you are going to waste everything and be a biker, is that it? Run drugs and fuck cheap whores. You won't have shit in that life."

"Being your bitch makes me better?" I snarl and step further into his space.

"If you are telling me no, then you need to understand that I'm not paying for your school, this apartment, none of it. Take that piece of shit cut off now, or you will be dead to me," he spits his threat and anger into my face.

"It ain't ever coming off," I taunt. "Do what you have to, asshole. I'm not having this conversation with you again. I don't need your prissy ass money or suits."

My dad's fists clench at his side. "Don't come fucking crying to me later. Remember, you made this shit the way it is."

I pull my cell and wallet out of my pocket and toss them up, hitting him in the chest. "Take it all, I don't give a fuck. Live your life how you want. Leave me to mine." The dead tone and my words hit their mark as the phone and wallet hit the floor between us.

He backs away toward the only way out of my apartment. With one last glare over his shoulder, he is out the door and my life. Leaving the phone on the floor, I stomp on it with my boot and pick up the wallet on my way out. I'll go spend his money on blow, booze and my brothers, fuck this asshole.

The sound of a car honking their horn at a truck wakes me from my daydream on the road, and I chuckle. God, those last few grand I had was a celebration of my freedom. We partied for days after that. Never did I hear from my parents again or get a birthday card. My mother was a cold bitch to begin with. I am fairly certain she hadn't planned on getting knocked up with me and didn't give a shit to have me. The old bastard probably made her, for appearances' sake.

It takes about six hours before we reach the town of Napa, California, where the money cleaning headquarters is located. It's a nice area if you're into money and have a lot of it to show off. Not my kind of place. We find a hotel and park the SUV at the entrance.

"I don't even want to know what this place costs a night," Axl comments, whistling low.

We had to dress in slacks and polos for the journey here, to mix in with the swanky crowd. I pull at the collar of my shirt, wishing I could tear this Eddie Bower shit off. After we settle into our room, we take a drive around and get a layout of the streets, getting an idea of how we can get in and out easily.

We park a few miles away from the property that belongs to the old man and wait for the sun to set. After, Axl and I dress in all black and we begin to sneak through the darkening vineyard field to get to the house. We listen carefully for guards, and not coming across any only confirms how laid back he is. Which is good, because he may not have figured out what we stole yet. Spider disabled his home security from back in Reno so that we could get in when we need to. We set up our stakeout location close to the house, up on a hill.

I watch closely around the property for movement before I spot them. It looks like the old man has some associates over. I'm sure they're just other assholes that he cleans money for. About an hour later, they shake hands and all but two guys leave. The three of them walk out to the patio by the pool where they have cigars lit and finish drinking what looks like scotch.

One guy takes off his tie, but that's not what makes me almost lose it. It's the guy next to him that tears away all of his clothes. I turn to Axl. "What the fuck is going on here?" I whisper shout from the bushes we're hiding behind. Turning back to the scene, I see that the two guys are naked now. One of them is on his knees taking the other in his mouth while my dad sits in his chair watching, puffing away at his cigar.

"Fuck, bro, your dad is *gay*," Axl snickers the obvious.

"I can't watch this right now," I groan. "We can come back tomorrow," I plead with him to let us leave.

"You can call Stryker and tell him why then," Axl laughs quietly.

"Fuck." I can't tell Stryker I left because of this. He'll kill me for being a pussy. "Tell me when it's over."

But no, Axl can't do that. That's what a good friend would do, but not him. He gives me the blow-by-blow, literally. "That dude that was sucking off that other guy is now blowing your old man. And the other guy is now ramming his ass from behind. These dudes are intense, *Jesus*."

He takes a break from talking but not for long. "Wowzah, your dad is now ramming the rammer, and that's some shit I'll need to wash from memory because, yep. Not what I was expecting, but I can't stop watching either."

"Can you shut the fuck up already?"

"There is nothing wrong with sexuality, *Lucas*." Axl uses my first name like he's reprimanding a little kid. He continues giving me the details until, *finally*, it is all over and dear old dad gets into a car and leaves for the night, I assume.

We backtrack over to our truck, and, as we jump in, I make a call to Stryker and Blade and inform them about the ass fucking crazy we found, and job not done for today.

"I don't know about going through with this, it seems odd to me. Where the hell is my mom? I think we should look closer into this before we take him out."

The line is quiet before Stryker replies, "We'll get the guys on it, but we stay on track. If I have to get Axl to pull the trigger, Tank, your ass will be the next that's fucked, you hear me?"

That could really mean almost anything coming from him. He could have the guys beat my ass down, strip me of my Road Captain patch, or of my cut completely. I won't fail my brothers. There is just something nagging at me to find out what it is.

CHAPTER 32

Kat

I knock a few more times but Tami doesn't answer, and I grow increasingly uncomfortable. Her car is in the driveway. Could she be napping or in the shower? I wait just a little longer and try knocking again, but nothing. Peeking through the side window, my eyes look around the house to see if I can find anything out of place, but it all seems too quiet.

Visions of a dead Tami and Cash flash before my eyes. I start panicking and pull my gun out from the bag. Quietly, I unlock the front door with my keys and pick Eli up from his stroller. I hold his sleeping body with one arm and rest his head in the crook of my neck.

My right hand is extended with the nine-millimeter and I begin searching the rooms one at a time. I start with the kitchen, then step into the living room area. I find Tami sitting on the couch and her eyes bug out right before a blood curdling screech leaves her mouth. The laptop on her knees flies to her left and she grabs her chest with one hand, ripping out her earbuds with the other.

"Kat, are you fucking crazy! Wait, you *are* fucking crazy if you came inside to kill people with your kid on your hip. Dude, you can't take a baby into a war!"

I lower the gun and set it on a side table next to the couch where Cash is sleeping next to where Tami was just sitting. Eli's head raises a bit from all the commotion, but he then drifts back to sleep.

"What the hell were *you* doing? I knocked forever— Hold on, I'm going to put Eli down." After I go to Tami's bedroom and lay Eli down on her bed, I come out only to face Tami, and I smirk at her annoyed face.

"God, you are dramatic. *Take your baby into war*," I tease her and pick Cash up from the couch to snuggle him to me. Tami sets her laptop down but turns the screen away from me. "What were you working on anyway? I thought you finished school?"

Tami's eyes dart around and won't look at me. Well, well, well, my lil' T has some secrets she's hiding, so when she ignores me and turns it around, I let her, for today.

"Yeah, school is done. But what the hell are you packing a gun around like that for? You scared the shit out of me."

I shrug a shoulder, "Old habits, I guess. I've carried a gun with me since I was fifteen. It feels like missing my wallet when I don't have it. At least you know I would save you, so there's that, and you are welcome."

"I'm telling Tank to take away all your guns. Seriously, you have to stop doing that, especially with Eli. Take care of him first, crazy lady."

Now that she said that, I do feel bad. "Damn. I think you're right. That was painful to say. But I came over to see what you were up to."

"You came over to check on me," Tami gives me a pointed look. "But thank you, I love you, too. It's the same, Kat. I just can't... I can't talk about it yet. I'm trying to work through it still." She holds onto the necklace around her neck and looks over at her computer.

"I'm here when you need me, okay?" I say, trying not to notice where her eyes went. The old me would remote log into her laptop within the next hour. I'm not going to kid you, I would love to see what she was up to, but I won't.

"Yeah, I know you are. How is your new life starting over?"

"Just trying to figure out who this new me is. I need something to do. I wish Blade would let me help at the MC with Spider, but that will never happen. Only other thing I can do is ask for a job at The Black Rose again. I don't think I'm ready to be out into the world, and, honestly, I don't know if I ever can be. It feels too weird and out of place."

"We have time."

Tami tries to smile through my words, and I decide that talking to her may be too selfish on my part. She doesn't have anything to give to others right now, *that* I can understand. She and I spend the afternoon together and I make her dinner before getting ready to head home with Eli.

I think we each have a hard time talking about the pain but being alone is even harder. Right before I am about to walk out with Eli in his stroller, she stops me. "Hey, *abuela* left this here for you. She wanted me to give it you when I saw you next."

Tami tucks a small envelope into my bag and waves goodbye as I walk down the sidewalk. This time, though, I walk with a purpose, ready to be back at the house. Quickly, I give Eli a bath and ready him for bed in his pj's.

The letter, I am almost sure of it, will bring me a rush of memories and pain. Eli lies next to me in my bed while I drink a glass of red wine and run my fingers through his hair, rubbing his back until he falls asleep. I finish two glasses before I have enough guts to open the envelope.

My fingers shake as I hold it in my hand. Taking a deep breath in, I finally flip it open. I pull out a photo and exhale the anguish of the picture trembling in my grip. My mother's timeless, beautiful smile along with mine fill the frame.

I can't pull my gaze away from the two of us together. My father burned every single thing she had made and every photo of her after she died. It was like she had never existed in our lives. The only thing left on this earth of her is gifted to me right now.

I look so much like her that my chest burns. I look at the next and it is of us playing in the yard, I would assume at *abuela*'s home. She must have saved these all these years for me when she knew I'd be ready to see them. I find her name in my contacts and hold the phone to my ear until she answers. Simply, I say softly, "*Gracias, abuela, te amo tanto.*"

"*Te amo tanto, mija.* You want to hear a story?" she questions with humor in her tone.

"*Sí.*"

I sit and listen to her tell me a long story of two young teenagers that ran away together because their love was so bold and strong. Their parents were so angry with them. Except for the father of the boy who had no remorse for what the kids had done. He was a strong and powerful man and used the situation to his advantage.

Over time, the greed destroyed the love of the two foolish kids, but not the love the mother had for her children who she fought to protect.

"Your mother would be so proud of you, Katherine. Forgive yourself of the choices you had to make to survive. She knows and will always love you unconditionally."

The words she says so easily are like a dagger to my heart, and I blink away the tears.

"Move on, *mija*, live and find a way to be at peace. Simply decide to be what you want. Live, because she wants you to."

"Okay. I'll call you soon." The words feel like razors but are all I can say.

"*Buenos noches. Buena suerte en tu viaje*, good luck on your journey, *mija.*"

I close my eyes and hold on tight to her words. Simply decide to be what I want.

I wake to a small hand that's tugging on my shirt. "Momma, wake!" One eye pops open to see Eli sitting on my stomach, drooling. "Eat now."

"Okay, sweet boy."

Sitting up, I take him with me and feed the early bird. That's when an idea hits me and I hurry to get us ready and out the door, which actually takes a few hours by the time I get to the store.

I hand over the small photo to the clerk and order a larger print that will be ready in an hour. Eli and I go to the store next door and we spend over two hours picking out new furniture to be delivered and other decorations to fill our house.

Together, we then pick up all the photos we ordered and stop at the grocery store for more food and drinks. I call in the troops. Let's do this housewife thing.

It doesn't take long before I have a houseful of women and kids. Harley, Emilia, Vegas, Jenn, Dana and Tami all show up to help give me a hand at being normal. The pizzas show up and we have beer and wine out for most and a few sodas for the rest and the kids.

Together, we laugh and stick photos into frames and I tell them stories of Tank that they never knew. Most of the pictures that are hung up are of Eli and Tank. My favorite is of them napping together up at the lake by the cabin. I even hang up the one of me and Eli at the park yesterday. The handful of them I have printed will go up, and I plan on taking many more until our home is filled with memories.

I take out the largest picture, the one of me with my mother, and place it in the center of the wall before we put the others up around it. The group of us grows quiet while we look at my mother's blown up, beautiful smile. "She was so beautiful."

"She is you," Jenn rasps next to me, I'm sure thinking of her own mother.

"They are us." In my head I whisper, *Love you, momma*, and know that, somewhere in heaven, she hears it.

Vegas and Dana are little machines and help to strategically place all the rest of the photos on the wall. When the store delivery truck shows up with everything else that I bought, we all pitch in to maneuver the furniture around the house. Curtains go up, the shelves are filled, and my house becomes a home. A new beginning.

CHAPTER 33

Tank

After that horrific show from late last night, I am happy to wake up in the hotel room where I have several text messages waiting for me from Kat. She and Eli are sitting on some furniture that she says she can't wait for me to see when I get home, along with everything else they have picked out.

It looks like whatever had her down yesterday, she is doing better with it today, and that makes me proud of her. While I am flipping through her pictures, I get a call from Spider.

"Yo, what did you find?"

"Your mom is living in California. It seems that she and your father split a while ago. I don't think you realize this, but he burned the shit out of her. Your mom was well off to begin with. He married her and then basically took her money, bro."

"You have got to be kidding me."

"Nah, it gets even better. He adopted you when you were one-year-old. That mother fucker ain't even your dad."

I have the phone on speaker, so Axl turns over from pretending to be asleep, even though it's a whole lot closer to noon. I sit up still dressed in my boxers, and leave the phone next to me on my bed.

I run my hands through my hair, "Are you sure? Because this feels so fucked up right now. I don't know, man, this is some Dr. Phil stuff straight off the T.V. kind of shit."

"I'm not wrong. He only wanted to keep you close, I'm sure, to get the rest of the money off your mom. Your grandparents left you a lot of cash that's sitting in an account that neither one of them can touch. That's why he was so pissed you chose the MC. He would have wanted you to invest."

"Transfer the fucking money to her, I don't want it. Can you send her flowers and say Happy fucking Mother's Day on them?" Axl and Spider chuckle at my request. "Was he working for Matias back then, too?"

"Yes, he's been on the Cartel's payroll for a long time. I'm going to keep digging, I'll be in touch."

The line goes dead and Axl sits up from across from me. "This just got that much easier."

"Fucking-A it did. I knew my mother was a piece of shit. If she does even know who my real father is, I don't give a fuck to know. Today did get that much easier. Let's find that piece of shit and get the fuck out of this place."

Axl nods with me in agreement. It takes us no time at all to get out the door and on the road to resolving my past. As soon as we reach his place in the beautiful hills of Napa, we park in the same spot as before and pull our black masks over our faces.

We trace our same steps from last night as we're sneaking back onto the property. He must be here because I hear music coming from somewhere inside the house. Carefully, with my gun drawn, I step inside from the back patio.

I find the piece of shit sitting behind the computer at his desk, typing away. Slowly, my feet glide across the floor undetected until I'm standing behind him.

Too distracted with his task, he has no idea that I am here. Raising my gun to a spot just above his head, I fire off a round. He startles and flies backward, grabbing his chest and swearing.

"Hello, dick, it's me." I walk around the desk and rip the mask away from my head, then look at the asshole square in the eyes.

"You're making a big mistake by being here," he threatens and leans forward. "You're dead. I should have drowned you in the bathtub when I had the chance."

Laughing at his words, I place my hands on his desk and tower over him, "Geez, *dad*, that's harsh and really hurts, *dick*. Especially since you *aren't* my dad. Now, wire transfer ten million to this account." I toss a folded piece of paper on the desk between us. His eyes flare before he scowls at me and then at the paper.

"Like hell I am transferring any fucking money. You are out of your goddamn mind if you think I'll give away ten million."

Axl walks into the room and, with a smirk, informs us, "House is empty."

"I didn't ask you to, I'm *telling* you to. Do it now, or the pictures of the midnight fuck fest will be sent out to all your associates. I'm assuming that was a private party," I state with a pleasant smile and a tilt to my head.

"Give me the photos and I will transfer the money," he demands and his fist slams down on the desk.

"No. Transfer the money, or, with one text, your shit goes viral."

Dear old dad's nose flares, his face turns red before he finally decides to listen. He snatches the paper off the desk and turns to his laptop, then follows the instructions to wire transfer the funds. Little does he know that he sent the money from Matias back to the other Cartel Bosses with his own money. Freeing them of any suspicions of where it could be hidden.

It will look like he committed suicide with the photos and evidence that Spider will spin around his sudden death, that he had been blackmailed by Matias in the first place to do his dirty work.

I round the desk that separates us, and, with gloved hands, I search through his drawers until I find what I am looking for, all while pointing the gun at his head.

I pull out his own handgun and grip the handle tightly. My elbow flies back before he's able to mutter a single word. Both of his hands grab a hold of his nose.

While he's busy holding his face, I place the gun under his chin and pull the trigger. His brains splatter out from the back of his head, spraying the room.

Picking up his hand, I wrap it around his gun and then let it drop by his side. Gripping his shoulders, I push them forward, leaving him face down on his desk, dead in his own office.

Axl makes a call to Spider that our target has been taken care of and that he has a green light to finish cleaning up this mess with the Cartel. We load up and haul ass out of there as soon as humanly possible.

"Can't wait till I get home," Axl comments on our way through the valley.

"Um, we have one more stop to make."

"Fuck, seriously? Where?"

I turn my head from the road for a second. "Jazz," is all I have to say and Axl moans regretfully.

"Will it take long? I was hoping to get home today."

"Hell if I know," I mutter and continue to drive like a bat out of hell until we reach Jazz's shop, which is conveniently located close to the clubhouse in Sacramento.

She owns and operates the Black Heart Tattoo shop. I called earlier and let her know we were on our way. Jazzy reschedules her customers for the Battle Born when we need her, she's cool as shit.

Walking into her studio, I whistle low at the classy modern feel. She must be raking in the cash by the looks of it, and good for her. "What's up, Jazz," I call out, searching around for her.

She steps out from the supply room and waves. "I drew up what you asked for, it's on my desk. Check it out! I'll be out in a few."

Just as she said, I find the stencil ready. There is the head of a black cat in the middle, similar to what a playboy bunny would look like. The top has Kit Kat written in fancy script. Simple and beautiful all at the same time, just like her.

"You like it?" Jazzy walks in, dressed in black, with her black and deep purple hair in a ponytail.

"Let's do it," I sit in her chair, all prepped and ready to go.

"All black?" she asks while cleaning and shaving my forearm.

"Wouldn't have it any other way."

She nods and spreads a cream over my skin before carefully placing the drawing onto my arm. The entire tattoo will take up about half of my left forearm. Jazzy gets to work, outlining and branding me for life with my woman's name.

By the time she's done, it has become my favorite tattoo to date, and I can't wait to show K-Love her new present and the other plan I have for her. I just need to make a quick call to Vegas for help.

CHAPTER 34

Kat

"You want to do *what*?" I shriek in disbelief.

Tank arrived home really late last night and he is now informing me that he has to pack another bag to leave today. I'm not even sure that I am awake yet. Can I be dreaming?

"What is that tattoo on your arm? Let me see that," I point to the fresh tattoo on his forearm. "What have you been doing these last few days?"

Tank holds out his arm and my fingers trace over the fresh tattoo. My eyebrow raises. "Kit Kat with a—"

"Pussy," he wiggles his eyebrows. "So all the girls know who my pussy is, baby."

"Sweet *and* thoughtful," I deadpan, but really, he is sweet and funny. I shake my head at him. His stupid face glows with pride for what he has done. He bends over and gives me a quick peck.

"I want you with me everywhere I go at all times. I wanted you to feel that you claimed me too."

Setting my coffee on the counter, I wrap my arms around him and place a kiss to his bare chest right over his heart, and hold on for just a moment.

"Pack your bags," Tank demands and walks away toward our room. "No guns or ammo, nothing like that. Sunscreen and bikinis only." He sounds beyond excited, throwing his clothes onto the bed. "Go, woman, pack now! It's a surprise." He walks over to me and places his soft lips over mine, whispering, "We don't know how much time will be given to us, and every chance I get to be happy, I'm doing it. Come with me?"

My hands hold onto his wrists. "Yes, of course I will follow you anywhere," I whisper back.

"Good, pack for fun." His grin makes me catch the same enthusiasm as him.

I can't stop the smile that breaks free from me. "A surprise with sunscreen and bikinis, huh?"

"Not telling you, woman, get in the car if you want to find out." He swats my ass and I laugh because I don't have a bikini, but I'll worry about that later. I grab the few things I do have to take with me.

Soon, we have the SUV packed with our stuff and we are on the road to a destination unknown. It's been hours now, and Eli is fast asleep in his car seat. My arm snakes across the middle console and I hold out my open hand for Tank to take. He removes his from the steering wheel and pulls it to his mouth, kissing the back before he rests our joined hands on his leg.

My surprise, I would guess, is a beach vacation since we are headed to California, and I can't love him more for it. I've never been on a vacation like this. It feels great to do something so easy. I get lost in the comfort of the road and the scenic drive down the coast.

Eventually, we make it to our destination, and I am shocked beyond belief. "You took us to Disneyland!"

He parks the SUV at one of the Disney resorts and tears fill my eyes. "Love you."

"Love you." Tank brings my face to his. "You made me long for adventure, long for you, here we are." He kisses my nose, "Get my boy out of the car and I'll meet you at the desk with our bags."

Eli and I enthusiastically look around with big eyes at a new world we have never seen before. I'm not sure, but I take a chance and tell the girl at the counter the reservation is under Lucas Taylor and pay for the room with a credit card.

Tank meets us at the desk after he helps loading the bags with the bellhop, and our clothes are taken up to the room. "Is Eli hungry?" he asks him with a raised brow.

"Yes," Eli pumps a fist into the air and almost loses his footing with the force of his man thrust. Tank's hand darts out and grips his, stopping him from falling to the slick tile floors.

We wander through the hotel until we find a cute diner and Eli asks for pancakes. I'm about to tell him no, but Tank's hand covers mine and orders a Mickey Mouse pancake with chocolate milk for them both. My head shakes but what can I do other than join them, so I order the same.

On our way back to the room, I find a gift shop and drag the boys in with me. I find us all bathing suits that match, with the Mickey Mouse logo on them. "Let's go to the pool?"

After the three of us are decked out in our family suites, we head up to the rooftop pool that has a mini playground with water slides. We spend hours chasing the sun and Eli in the water. Eventually, he's so tired, he curls up on Tank and passes out. Tank holds him tight and places a kiss on his head. I capture the perfect moment with my phone camera to add it to our picture wall later.

We spend the next two days riding every ride possible and eating all the food you can imagine. The park is beyond huge, but I enjoy every second of our fun adventure. It really is the happiest place on earth.

On the third day, I suggest we try something different. "Would you like to go to the beach today?"

Tank walks out from the bathroom. "Not today, but later we will definitely go to the beach." He steps a little closer. "You have a spa day planned and the boys have their own day."

"Hmm, a spa day, I couldn't possibly say no."

"Good, because the girls will be here any second."

"What girls?" There's a knock at the door and I run to see if it is who I think it is. All the girls from home are standing outside the door, waiting for me. I blow a kiss to my boys on my way out and eagerly leave with the girls.

First, we get pedicures and manicures. It's been such a long time since I had the time to take care of myself, and I love every second of it. We have the best lunch with Mimosas or Bloody Mary's. We laugh and tell jokes and it's great to see even Tami loosen up a little.

"Where are all the kids at?" I ask looking at all of them.

"You won't believe this! The guys have them all up in the room. Tank called this morning and said he needed a nap day. So, the guys have a nap day planned," Vegas laughs. "That doesn't sound bad, though, because we never sleep anymore."

"They even have Cash with them. It's all bikers and babies," Dana chuckles. "That must be the cutest sight."

I laugh and glance at Tami. She doesn't hear Dana, and her forlorn look tells me she is off in another world. Time, she needs a little more time and she'll come around.

After lunch, we get deep tissue massages that are heaven on this earth. I am so relaxed that I don't even notice the clothing rack they wheeled in which is filled with white dresses at first.

My hands grip the robe at my chest even tighter, "What is going on here?"

Harley's eyes glitter with mischief. "Your wedding is tonight. We are going to pick you a beautiful dress."

"That sneaky— I can't even cuss here! He took me to the one place on earth where I can't shoot him. I *told* him that I didn't want a wedding."

Jenn's evil eyes look at me. "Maybe he knew deep down that you did," she points a finger at my chest, "and made you get out of your head to make it happen in the most magical kingdom on earth. Go with it and get a dress on, time's a-wastin'."

Slowly, I get up from the couch and tiptoe over to the rack, then look through them all before one in particular sticks out to me. It's a long, silky ivory dress that has a deep V in the front. It's not the typical wedding dress, but it is beautiful.

With the spaghetti straps, it is quickly altered in a few places. It's amazing what money can buy, and, within hours, I'm ready. The girls all found similar dresses to the one I had picked, even down to the ivory heels.

My hair and makeup are professionally done. The hairdresser wraps my long black hair up into a classic updo, the makeup artist gives me a smoky eye with a light cat eye liner. I've never felt more gorgeous, and I know it is because of Tank's love.

They know where we are going and lead me to a lit garden that's on the hotel grounds. It's dark outside and there are white lights strung up everywhere. The scent of the flowers fills the air.

Blade is standing by the walkway and takes my arm. "Can I walk you down the aisle?" His gruff nature is put away for the night.

"Yes, thank you." Vegas, Jenn, Dana and Tami walk past us.

When he turns, the view opens, and Tank is standing there in an all-black tux under an arch covered in white flowers. It's elegant in all black and white. Timeless and romantic. My heart skips in my chest when Blade takes a step toward him. Spider, Axl and Saint stand to his left. Opposite them stand Tami, Dana, Jenn, and then Vegas at the end to where I will be standing.

I follow Blade's lead because I can't take my eyes off Tank. His hair has been trimmed and styled. He even had his beard trimmed and it looks sharp. A photographer stands off to the side and I notice the first picture being taken, but once I reach Tank and our hands meet, I lose sight of my surroundings and the outside world blurs, leaving only us.

An elderly man officiates the ceremony, holding a Bible. "Do you, Emily Scott, take Lucas Taylor to be your lawfully wedded husband in sickness or in health, until death do you part?"

"Yes, I do." Tami hands me a thick gold band to place on Tank's finger.

"Do you, Lucas Taylor, take Emily Scott to be your lawfully wedded wife in sickness or in health, until death do you part?"

"Yes, I take her to be my lawfully wife, Emily Scott," Tank's eyes smile, "Until death do us part..." and he bites his lip to keep from ruining the whole ceremony. My eyes squint because, if looks could kill, they would, but they say, *Don't you dare*. He wants to laugh at the *lawfully* marrying me, *Emily Scott*, until the death part, or both. Probably both.

He slides a thin gold band on my ring finger and squeezes my hand.

"You may now kiss your bride."

Tank tugs me to him and dips me backward, "Forever the light in my life."

CHAPTER 35

Tank

"Kat, get up, it's time to hit the road." My palm runs down her side and to the back. Her skin feels like silk to the touch. I reach her ass and give it a soft squeeze. She moans lightly and lifts her leg to wrap it over mine, exposing her pussy to me.

In the early morning rays, on the day after we got married, she is still hungry for more. My fingertips caress her clit soft and slow, waking her mind up as well as her body. I need and crave her lust as much as I need my next breath. Dipping my fingers inside her cunt, I bring them back up to her clit, caressing her.

"Fuck, Tank, after all last night, I didn't think you could get me there again so soon," she moans when I nip and kiss her neck down to her shoulder.

"I want to feel you come on my cock all the time." Pushing my pelvis forward, I enter her wet, hot pussy, and this time I'm the one moaning as I rock back and forth slowly. I can't stop myself from the abys she pulls me into every time she is close. "I want to wrap you up and call you mine forever. I'll never let you forget it."

Kat's hand comes up and snakes around my head. Her nails scrape my skin on their journey. She turns her body over, opening herself more to me. She makes me feel wanted and needed just by doing that. Kat always finds ways to show me her love.

She's close and her chest heaves. "I will fall apart without you." She untangles herself from me and forces me on my back with a light touch to my chest. I roll over and let her take control. Kat straddles me and takes me slowly into her. Her head falls back and her long black hair cascades down, reaching my legs while she rocks her body up and down.

My hands glide up her thighs to her tits, cupping them. She picks up her pace and my dick reacts to her aggressivity, my balls drawing up. "Rub your pussy for me, baby."

Kat reaches down and circles her clit with fast strokes. She's ready and needs so much more. My hands grip her waist and I pound her as hard as she can take from below her.

Her head flies back again as she releases her orgasm for me. I go off with my wife and hold her to me, coming inside my woman. She rocks her hips just how I need it, allowing me to come down with her.

Kat leans forward and takes my face in her hands, fucking my mouth with her tongue. "Love you," she rasps against my lips.

My hands squeeze her ass. "Kat, there is nowhere else I want to be but right here with you, fighting for you and our family forever. I love you."

She grinds against me again, wanting more of me. My chest is full of emotion. Kat learned that I would always love her and never hurt her. Every touch between us means something. Every time we are like this together, it's our safe place. This is how we share our love and always will.

"K-Love, I would love nothing more than to fuck you dirty and hard right now, but I have other plans for today. We have to hit the road," I playfully smack her ass. "Get up! It's time to shower and pack a riding bag."

Kat goes along with it, and I fucking love it so hard, because that makes me happy to surprise her. After our shower, Axl shows up to take Eli from us. That is, after Kat is done kissing every inch of his face.

"Bye, lil' E, be a stud. We'll be home soon." He waves back and says *Bye, daddy* and my heart explodes in my chest. My fist raises and he gives me his knuckles. "You are the king, kid."

Axl's eyes squint, "Let's not fight about that in front of the kid. C'mon, dude, we have to get a few things straight. On our ride back." This time, Kat squints and places her hands on her hips, looking like she's about to say something, but ends up laughing instead and dropping it for now.

On his way out, Axl tosses my bike keys and I toss him the Suburban keys. He'll come by later and load our stuff, and a prospect will drive it all back to Reno for us.

Kat and I grab our bags and begin our honeymoon. Hand in hand, we find my bike in the parking lot garage, and I hold my hand for her to sit behind me. She slides in close and wraps her arms around my body. Looking down, I see the diamond on her ring finger sparkling in the sun. She is home, right where she is supposed to be, at my side. I have it all.

I could have taken Kat anywhere in the world. But, right now, her world is Eli, so a ride up the Coast for a few days, sightseeing the beaches, was the best idea.

I rev the engine up and we start the first day of the rest of our lives as a family, wrapped up completely in our love. We coast up the scenic highway of California and stop every day in random places. Wherever she wants to go, I let her navigate.

The only thing I wanted to see was my wife in her Mickey Mouse bikini at the beach every day, and I got that and more. Never again will I doubt the journey and obstacles in front of me. I'll always trust the path and know that the road ahead of me was given to me for a reason.

Never stop fighting for what is right or believing that you deserve more.

Be brave and be Battle Born.

Fighting for forever.

THE END

BONUS SCENE

Tank

Kat struggles at first to slide out of the car. She loves her Tesla. I've been trying to convince her to get a bigger vehicle due to our growing family. She's holding on to the bitter end.

I quickly hop out of the driver's side and run around to give her a hand and pull her up to me. My hand comes down and rubs her belly.

"How's my girls?"

"We don't know that the baby is a girl, Tank." She's cranky, too, from the heat and being pregnant and miserable all summer.

Kissing her forehead, I whisper, "I *know*, K-Love. Only a woman can drive a person this mad." She pushes me back and I laugh at her.

She opens the back door and helps Eli out for his first day of kindergarten, then places a backpack on his shoulders. Her hand goes to touch his head and mine snaps out to stop her. "Woman, we spent a lot of time on that mohawk for the ladies. He needs to look like a badass. Leave the boy be."

I squat down next to Eli and face us toward the school. "Take our picture?" Together we pose for a few funny pics, then I pick Eli up and pull Kat to us for a selfie before we walk him inside.

"Look tough, E, until you know who the players in the room are, and *then* make your friends. This is an important step. You have your whole school career ahead of you. And today is day one. Set yourself up right today, you got me?"

"Got you, big T! I got this!" Eli's eyes get hard and he walks into the room with swagger. He nods at his teacher and tosses his bag into a cubby like he owns it. Before the door shuts, he turns around and pumps his fist, then struts over to his assigned desk.

Kat covers her mouth and starts talking through her laughter, "How many times have you practiced that, Tank? That was *not* my baby in there."

I raise a brow, "That was not a *baby*, that was a little dude learning to be a big dude. This is my business, woman. You don't become like this," I point up and down my body with one finger, "Without some practice. And I'll never tell what we do. That's man business. Know your role, momma."

"You're fucking kidding me, right?" Kat's voice drops low as we walk out. Another mother hears it and glares at her words as she pushes her daughter to walk faster and away from us. Kat's about to tell the mom off, I can tell, so I push her away as fast as possible, too. She is a damn time bomb filled with aggression. Hot, hot lil' momma.

"Let's go get some frozen yogurt?" I prompt.

"Stop trying to save people from me!" she stomps to the car. "I'm not going to kill anyone."

"Calm down, Kitty Kat. I can't spank your ass, so calm down."

Kat glares at me from the other side of the car. "If you think that by telling me," every word she says gets a little louder than the last, "To calm the hell dow—" She bends forward and holds her stomach. "Ouch, fuck me."

I run to meet her on the other side of her car. "Are you okay?" I ask, rubbing her back.

"Oh shit, my water broke." She looks up at me with teary eyes. "It's time?"

"Yeah, K-Love, let's take you and Blake to the hospital."

She takes in a deep breath through her nose and then exhales slowly through her mouth. "I thought you said it was a girl."

"The B's of life, babe. Now get your leaking ass into the car." She glares at me while I laugh at her as I go back on the driver's side. I feel her eyes like lasers on me the entire time.

"What is so fucking funny, Tank?"

Putting the car into drive, I answer, "We are getting a new SUV now that you got your birthing stuff all over this one."

Kat's face is so red, she's about ready to blow, but, thankfully, a contraction hits her right then. I drive as fast as I can all the way to the hospital. Surprisingly, I'm not pulled over and absently think that no cop would want to deal with this. It's as if they somehow knew.

The nurses help me to get Kat and our baby girl set up in a private room as soon as we arrive. I called ahead and paid extra for her because she is a demon.

Kat is then stripped down and dressed into a hospital gown. She bites the nurse's head off for missing her vein when they try to put the IV needle in. The nurse runs out, excusing herself to get Kat some ice chips. But I saw the fear in her eyes. My woman is scary.

I send Tami and Blade a quick text to let them know that Kat is having the baby. Kat's sniffling surprises me and I walk over to her. "What's wrong, K-Love?"

"I'm scared, Tank." She sniffles again.

"Because you have to shoot a baby out of that vagina, girl? You *got* this, just like Eli does. Be brave, little momma."

"Tank, have you seen the size of your head?!"

I try, and fail, to hold back the grin that creeps over my face, then the all teeth smile that takes complete control. "Kat, it's a girl. She'll have your head. What are you so worried about?"

Another contraction hits her hard followed by several more for the next hour. The doctor finally comes in and pales, getting his staff ready for delivery. Tami comes barreling around the corner and is at Kat's side in seconds, holding her hand. "We are having a baby today!" she exclaims.

The doctor's eyes bug out in confusion and I'm not too humble to let him think that they are my lesbian wives. Yep, not too humble at all.

Tami and I hold Kat's hands as she screams bloody murder from having a natural childbirth. First, the head comes out and I am fascinated by what my wife can do. I help her as best as I can, holding her leg up to her chest as she pushes our baby out. Just like Kat, she screams. Yep, *she* screams when the doctor has her in his hands and rests her on my K-Love's chest.

"Hey, baby Blake Maria Taylor."

Kat's lower lip quivers, "I love that name."

"Your mom is a part of her, too." My hand runs over the baby's tiny body which is just a tad bigger than my hand.

The nurse takes Blake from Kat to finish cleaning her and the doctor gives her an exam before I give her a bath. "Kat, I gave Blake her first bath."

"Idiot, they're all yours. Congratulations."

We settle in after that and Kat falls asleep exhausted when Eli comes in with Blade and Vegas, his godparents. Eli washes his hands and walks over to give his sister an adoring kiss.

"She's your responsibility, too. You have to take care of her and protect her for the rest of your life, lil' E." He points at his chest. "Yep, Blake is *your* 'little' now."

Family is team building, and nothing on this earth could make me happier than Kat and our babies. The B's of life...

WHAT'S COMING NEXT?

Loving You Forever, Pawn's Story...

Pawn spent every one of his days on the inside fighting to survive. All that got him through was counting the minutes until he could hold his son for the first time. Can Pawn beat his own demons and addictions to become the father his baby needs?

Tami's heart is broken. Following Solo's death, she doubts she will ever be loved again. First, she must find her own voice and gain the courage to be alone.

But when mistakes from Tami's past hunt her down, she learns a harsh lesson about trifling with thieves. Proving his feelings for her never diminished, Pawn rushes in to protect her. Will he sacrifice himself to save his family?

Or stand tall as the hero he never thought he could be?

TO THE READERS

Holy shit we made it to the end! I didn't know that I would love Tank as much as I do. When I started his character, way back in book one, I had no idea who I would end up with. A man as deep as the ocean. He's funny, loyal, brave and so loving. Real. I fell in love with him more and more with every word. He really is my favorite male character. He snuck up on me and caught me without me even realizing it, lol, kind of like what he did to Kat too.

Katherine, the Black Widow to Kat or K-love and also known as Kit Kat or Kitty Kat, she evolved the most out of my girls. At least I thought so. She came from an abusive life and Tank taught her to love because she was open to change and ultimately evolved into the woman, I think she always wanted to be, her mother. Or a mother and as close as she could. I love her hard exterior but has a brave and loyal heart underneath. I love her very much too.

Every book, I put my whole heart into every word. By the end I feel so much. So happy that I could cry because I made it. So sad because it is over, and I am going to miss the friends I just wrote about. Just drained from expressing every emotion possible from anger to laughing and everything in between. I write in hopes that I give you a book that you will hopefully enjoy and touch your heart and mind.

Be brave, be beautiful and most of all, fight for what you deserve. Everything.

~Scarlett.

ABOUT THE AUTHOR

Scarlett Black is the author of the Battle Born MC Series. Not really knowing where a story will take her is what she loves most about writing. She strives to write about strong women and the men who love them. She believes in love and the miracles that come from it. She enjoys giving her fans a happily ever after worth melting their hearts. These may be books, but they are written with her heart and soul. She is Battle Born. Are you?

www.authorscarlettblack.com

Made in the USA
Columbia, SC
14 November 2020

24565278R00141